Hoofbeats

Margret and Flynn, 1875

by KATHLEEN DUEY

DUTTON CHILDREN'S BOOKS

DUTTON CHILDREN'S BOOKS
A division of Penguin Young Readers Group

Published by the Penguin Group
Penguin Young Readers Group,
345 Hudson Street, New York, New York 10014, U.S.A.
Penguin Group (Canada), 90 Eglinton Avenue East, Suite 700, Toronto, Ontario
Canada M4P 2Y3 (a division of Pearson Penguin Canada Inc.)
Penguin Books Ltd, 80 Strand, London WC2R 0RL, England
Penguin Ireland, 25 St Stephen's Green, Dublin 2, Ireland
(a division of Penguin Books Ltd)
Penguin Group (Australia), 250 Camberwell Road, Camberwell, Victoria 3124,
Australia (a division of Pearson Australia Group Pty Ltd)
Penguin Books India Pvt Ltd, 11 Community Centre, Panchsheel Park,
New Delhi - 110 017, India
Penguin Group (NZ), 67 Apollo Drive, Rosedale, North Shore 0632,
New Zealand (a division of Pearson New Zealand Ltd)
Penguin Books (South Africa) (Pty) Ltd, 24 Sturdee Avenue, Rosebank,
Johannesburg 2196, South Africa

Penguin Books Ltd, Registered Offices: 80 Strand, London WC2R 0RL, England

This book is a work of fiction. Names, characters, places, and incidents
are either the product of the author's imagination or are used fictitiously,
and any resemblance to actual persons, living or dead, business
establishments, events, or locales is entirely coincidental.

The publisher does not have any control over and does not assume any
responsibility for author or third-party websites or their content.

CIP DATA IS AVAILABLE.

Published simultaneously by Dutton Children's Books and Puffin Books,
divisions of Penguin Young Readers Group
345 Hudson Street, New York, New York 10014
www.penguin.com/youngreaders

Printed in USA · First Edition

10 9 8 7 6 5 4 3 2 1

ISBN 978-0-525-47936-9

For Ty Tyson. Thank you for encouraging me to ride bare-back and barefoot—backward, forward, and sideways. Thank you for teaching me how to understand the flick of a horse's ear, a tail-switch, a tightness of stance, a tiny shift of weight. Thank you helping me feel a horse's uneasiness, fear, happiness, excitement, shyness—and best of all—trust.

CHAPTER ONE

❧ ❧ ❧

On Independence Day, I went to the well before sunup. Mrs. Frederiksen's place is on a little rise. Not much of one, but it's all flat as johnny cakes out to the east, so I could see all the way to the horizon in that direction. And I saw something. I just couldn't see *clear*. I squinted in the dawn dusk at a blurry darkness roiling above the grassland. I couldn't smell smoke, but the breeze was blowing the wrong way.

Maybe it was dust? I hoped so. We'd had no rain for a few weeks. It was probably dry enough for a cattle drive to kick up a brown cloud, if the herd was big enough.

I didn't want it to be smoke. Smoke meant fire, and if it was a big fire, we'd have to run for it and then we might end up never coming back here again. Libby took almost any excuse to move on.

She liked roaming—staying two steps ahead of trouble, she called it. I didn't. I liked it when we stayed in one place for a while. And I liked Mrs. Frederiksen more and more. Libby didn't trust her. But Libby almost never trusted anyone.

I pulled in a long breath. No smoke smell yet. I wanted to wait a few minutes, see if the breeze would change once the sun was up. But I knew if I stood there much longer, Libby would get upset with me for dawdling. I set the full water bucket by the path, then ran for the barn.

Mrs. Frederiksen had let her wheat fields go fallow and had sold off all her cattle. But she still kept a big garden and had a milk cow named Bessie and two horses, Bennie and Tish. The horses woke and nickered when they heard me slide the barn door back. I lit the lantern and hung it up, then said good morning to them both. They were pretty bays, calm and sweet the way horses always are if someone is kind to them. And Mrs. Fredericksen was. She was old, but she was still sort of pretty, with high cheekbones and long, slim-fingered hands that were graceful, no matter what chore she was doing. Her hair was so long that she never wore it down, instead twisting and winding it into an intricate bun.

The first day we met her, she'd told us that she was a widow who had raised two sons and a daughter.

Only the daughter was still alive, raising her own family in Denver City now. I had never asked Mrs. Frederiksen anything more about her sons and I never would. Neither would Libby. We were the last two to pester anyone to talk about their sorrows.

On our second day with her, I had asked Mrs. Frederiksen if I could ride her horses. She had stared into my eyes, made me promise to be careful, not to hurt myself or the horses. Then she had said that her husband had ridden often, to check the wheat fields, to visit a neighbor, to go to town. But she didn't go much of anyplace anymore—only a few times a year in the wagon to Littleton for dry goods. "Bennie is old. But Tish loves a good gallop," she told me. "I'd be happy if she got one now and then."

The first time I took Tish out, I discovered there was only one saddle in the barn. The cinch was old and frayed, and one of the stirrup leathers had rotted and split. So I rode bareback—which I liked better anyway. Tish really did like to gallop still, especially in the cool of morning or evening. She was a little uneasy with me riding bareback at first, but had gotten used to it. Libby hated me riding, but she didn't forbid me partly because she knew how much I loved it and partly because she could see how placid and calm Tish was. A baby could have ridden her.

Libby had always been afraid of horses. I was the opposite. They all felt like old friends to me. Everywhere we had ever lived, I had ridden every chance I got. Something about riding eased my heart and made me happy. My dearest hope was to one day have a horse of my own.

I had told Libby that, just once. She had explained, in a voice that made me feel small and stupid, that we could barely feed ourselves. Much less a horse. And she forbade me to bring it up again.

Every morning, I led Bennie and Tish out to graze in the rail-fenced pasture. This morning, I watched them for a moment as I slid the fence rails back into place, closing them in. Neither of them acted the least bit nervous. They were breathing deep and slow, grazing without lifting their heads to look around for danger. So it wasn't smoke—or the wind was so far wrong that not even they could smell it yet. I went back to the barn and tossed Bessie some of the dried grass piled outside her stall, then poured a half pail of cracked corn into her manger.

I walked back toward the little sod house, the ding-dang water bucket dripping on my right shoe all the way. I kept glancing at the horizon, squinting, wishing the sun would hurry up. I thought I could still see the dark place. Maybe not. It had been a mile or two off—whatever it was. Maybe farther. So even if it was smoke, the fire might not come close unless the wind came up. Would the soddy burn? I didn't see how it could. It was built from scraped-up slabs of dirt, held together by the roots of the wiry grass that covered the prairie. Mrs. Frederiksen told me that she and her husband had cut the squares and stacked them like oversize bricks years before. The soddy roof had timbers, but they were covered in the sod, too. I stared into the dusky distance for one more long moment, standing on the porch. I couldn't see even a glimmer of fire shine. It had to be dust.

When I pushed open the unlatched door, my sister was bent over, blowing the hearth fire back to life, raking the coals to one side to bake bread later. Our bedding was neatly folded in the far corner and she had swept the planked floor. There was a mound of brownish dough on the sideboard. My mouth watered. There would be fresh sourdough bread in a few hours. My sister was a very good cook. I set down the bucket beside the little pine-board dresser that held the skillets and pot rags and waited for Libby to finish. She didn't like being interrupted at anything she was doing.

Mrs. Frederiksen was still abed in her room, walled off from the rest of the soddy by rough

plaster walls. She slept later than we did some-
times, but not by much. I wasn't sure how old
she was. Her hair was white. And her daughter,
Colleen, was her youngest, she had said that much.
She said Colleen visited sometimes, but not nearly
often enough now that she was married to a Denver
City banker and had two children of her own. Mrs.
Frederiksen hadn't sounded upset saying that,
but kind of sad. They were lovely children, Mrs.
Frederiksen told us. Sweet-natured, and a joy.

Staring at my sister, waiting for her to turn
around, I thought about that. Banker's kids. What
would that be like, living in a big house, staying
put, not going off somewhere new two or three
times a year?

My sister straightened up and saw me standing
there, waiting. She made an impatient gesture.
"What?"

"I saw something, Libby."

She frowned and shook her head and made
the gesture again.

"There's dust," I told her. "I think. Or smoke.
Come look."

Libby straightened her shoulders. "Close?"

I shook my head. "A mile or two off to the east.
Maybe three or four. I can't tell—the sun is barely
up. Could be buffalo dust."

I watched her nudge the kindling farther back in the hearth, then she hung the log hook on the wall rack. When she turned to face me again, she shooed me with her hands. "Don't stand and gawp at me, Margret. If there's something to worry about, we'll know soon enough. Go get firewood, I need to wash our clothes today."

"But it's only Saturday," I said.

"Monday's laundry includes the bedding," she told me, and I needed no further explanation. Bedding would be backbreaking enough, without clothes added in. So I went back out, headed for the woodshed this time, wishing Libby would come look at the dust or whatever it was. But I knew better than to argue with her—it was like arguing with a rock.

Going up the path, I wished Libby would stop acting like I was still a baby. She was seventeen, six years older than me, and the only family I had ever had. She had been seven when we were orphaned. I had been a few months shy of turning two. I can't remember our parents at all. I have tried—oh, I tried so hard. But I just couldn't. Libby wouldn't tell me anything, either.

When I first started asking, Libby had said it didn't matter all that much. Then she would pepper me with questions. We had stayed clear of

Mr. Lincoln's war, hadn't we? We had stayed safe and sound in Iowa, hadn't we? And we were making our way all right, just two of us, weren't we? And all that was true. But I still wanted to know about our parents.

Mrs. Frederiksen's little sod shed was stacked full of split pine logs, cut to stove length. There were no pine trees within ten miles or more. In fact, there were hardly any trees at all except for the cottonwoods along the river, and cottonwood doesn't hold a coal much longer than twisted paper. Mrs. Frederiksen had told us the wood had been freighted in by a man who brought it from somewhere west of Denver and had cut, split, and seasoned it. Mrs. Frederiksen's daughter had drawn him a map, and paid him to haul it here, stack it in the shed, then go back to Denver. She had arranged the same thing the year before, too.

Mrs. Frederiksen saying that made me feel like I had seen a pig fly past. How much money do you have to have to feel like you can spend it on something as silly as that? The rest of the settlers along this stretch of the South Platte River burned wood from trees they'd planted for the purpose, or they still did what the first settlers had done. They burned dried buffalo and cow dung for winter warmth, and all year, to cook, too. It worked fine. On any clear day, I could see three other farmhouses from Mrs. Frederiksen's chicken coop on the south side of the soddy. And as long as we had been there, I had seen specks moving in long zigzags across the cow pastures and the unfenced land—it was the littlest children in each family, stopping, bending, walking again—they were picking up buffalo and cow chips.

Mrs. Frederiksen wasn't young, but she was tough as saddle leather and she could have picked up her own buffalo chips. She could carry a feed sack of buffalo patties all day and not be weary. Almost anybody could. They aren't heavy. Or she could fashion a little pannier rig for Tish or Bennie, either one would welcome the exercise and the diversion. And Mrs. Frederiksen wouldn't have minded. She worked hard at something or other all day long. The wood was her daughter's idea, and I was pretty sure I knew why. Colleen and her family lived in Denver City—and she almost never came to visit. She probably felt bad and wanted to do something for her mother. And she probably worried, too, knowing that Mrs. Frederiksen was out here on her own.

I looked to the east on my way back up the hill. The smoke—or whatever it had been—was gone, and now that the sun was above the horizon, I could see that the sky was pocked with gray clouds.

"Maybe laundry should wait, I think it's a storm blowing in," I told my sister as I walked back into the kitchen. She was kneading the dough, rocking back and forth as she worked. She half turned and jutted her chin out, pointing at the hearth. "I'll go look in a minute," she said, slapping the dough. "Would you get the Dutch oven greased up for me? Then go milk."

I did as I was told. I always do. Greasing the cast-iron pot took two minutes, then I was back outside. Bessie was glad to see me. I milk fast. We had lived on a dairy farm—back in Nebraska. The Dannens sold milk and made cheese, and the whole family rose before light to start milking, including us. I had thought, at first, that we had finally found a home. They needed hands and we needed a place. And they were nice enough to us. The trouble was between the two of them. Mrs. Dannen told us the story in fits and starts.

When the army had come in and the Indian troubles had started again, she had wanted to go back east. Her husband didn't, so they stayed, but she was always scared. When statehood had come, they had disagreed about who should be able to vote, too, white men only, or all men. So they both worked dawn to dark, barely speaking. It was a silent, unhappy house. One day, Mrs. Dannen scolded Libby hard for a small thing. That night, Libby woke me up and we left by the light of the summer moon.

Libby likes leaving places at night. That way there is no argument. No one has ever found us. Maybe no one ever looked.

I walked up the hill with the pail of warm milk, and when I came in the door, Libby was bent over her bread dough still. Once I had the milk strained and cooling, she turned to face me.

"Go gather up the eggs." She sounded irritated. At me?

I smiled at her. "We'll have everything done by noon at the rate we're going."

"Go!" she said, shooing me with her flour-whitened hands. "If it rains, we'll be glad of it!"

"I can get the eggs." Mrs. Frederiksen's voice came down the narrow hall. A moment later she came into the kitchen. She pushed my hair back over my ears and kissed the top of my head. "Good morning, dearie." She had done it every morning since we'd shown up at her door, asking to trade a meal or two for a little work, but it still amazed me. I saw Libby glance at us sidelong. She always gets wary if anyone is too nice to us.

"We need to start putting up more hard cheese," Mrs. Frederiksen said, looking at the milk. She had been saying that since we had arrived. It was true. Bessie gave more milk than the three of us use. Curds soured before we could eat them all. Hard cheese kept a lot longer.

"And how are you this morning?" Mrs. Frederiksen asked Libby.

My sister had turned back to the bread dough. She said, "I am fine, thank you," without so much as looking over her shoulder. I wished she would try to be nicer, this once, just a little. So far, I liked it here.

"Well, I am glad to hear that, Miss Elizabeth Quinn," Mrs. Frederiksen answered, using my sister's whole name. Then she winked at me. "Shall we go annoy the chickens?"

I ran to get the egg basket from its hook on the wall. The clothesline rope was coiled next to it. I reached for it.

"Don't bother with that if it looks like rain," Libby said. "You still have one clean dress?"

I shook my head. "Just my good one."

"Try not to wallow in the mud, then," Libby said. "I want to make a special supper for Independence Day and I want you clean as possible at the table."

Mrs. Frederiksen gestured and we tiptoed out. Once we were outside, she stopped, as she always did, and stood very still, facing west. Then she lifted both of her hands, palms up, slanted toward the sky, and just stood there for a long moment, looking at the Rocky Mountains in the distance.

I knew what was coming. She let out the long breath and doubled at the waist, folding up like a jackknife. Then she straightened again and lifted her hands skyward once more. She did it three times, then breathed long and slow as she straightened.

"Aren't you ever going to ask me?"

I blinked. "I didn't want to be rude."

She shook her head. "Nothing rude about healthy curiosity. An Oriental fellow I met in California taught me. He said it would make me live longer. All I know is that it sets me right, every morning."

I had no idea what to say to that. Mrs. Frederiksen wasn't like anyone else I had ever known. She and her husband had gone all the way to California during the Gold Rush of '49, then had come back to Colorado Territory to homestead. If he had lived, she had told me, they were going to go on up to Oregon Territory to see some kind of red-wooded trees that were ten times the size of a big pine. She hadn't looked like she was joking.

"You are supposed to face east, toward the sun," she said. "I face west because William's grave is up there, on the far side of the pasture. He was my sun for thirty-five years." She paused and smiled. "And now you know why I cannot live in any other house, and I cannot move to Denver the way Colleen wants me to. I can't leave William."

Her voice was so full of love that I could not form a single thought for a moment. Then, when I did, it was not one thought, but four or five. I wished her husband was still alive. Then I felt glad that he wasn't. If he had been, she might not have taken us in so easily. And of course the instant I thought that, I felt terrible. How could I be that selfish?

"What are you thinking, Miss Margret?" she asked me as we walked around the end of the porch to the far side of the soddy. The chicken coop was built against the south-facing wall.

I had no idea what to say again. I wasn't really thinking anything. And what I had felt was too strange to try to explain. She glanced at me and I blinked and blushed a little. Then a low roll of thunder made us both look eastward.

"Storm coming," she said. "From the southeast, and black clouds, so it'll likely be a whopper."

I nodded. "I thought I saw smoke this morning. Or buffalo dust." I described the odd dark shape I had seen in the dawn-dusk.

She tipped her head and raised her eyebrows. "I wonder if you saw a tornado. It's certainly late in the season to get one." She looked back eastward and I felt my heart thudding in my chest. I had never seen a tornado and I didn't want to see one now.

"Let's get the eggs in," Mrs. Frederiksen said. "Sometimes when there's one tornado, there's more."

I nodded and went into the coop, sliding my hand beneath each hen as gently as I could. We found nine eggs and Mrs. Frederiksen smiled. "Nine! We could make a cake for tonight's supper and still have enough for breakfast tomorrow." I smiled back at her, but she wasn't looking at me. She was looking up at the sky.

An hour later, Mrs. Frederiksen had me put the horses back in the barn. By noon, the sky had turned black and lightning crackled overhead. The clouds were so dark and the downpours of rain so heavy that even with the oil lamp lit, the little sod house was almost midnight dark.

Except when the lightning flashed.

Then blue-white light knifed though every tiny slit in the sod walls and the gaps around the door frame, flashing against the little wax-paper window over the sideboard. And then, of course, the thunder came. Twice the lightning hit close by and the thunder shook the packed earth beneath the floor planks.

My sister sat in one of the kitchen chairs, her hands in her lap, her mouth set in a thin, tight line.

"Libby?"

She looked at me but didn't answer.

"We will be all right, won't we?"

She nodded and made the motion with her hands that meant I was to leave her alone. I hated it, sometimes, but I knew that if I kept trying to talk to her, she would just get angry, so I hushed.

The oil lamp flickered, but there was nothing cheery about the little flame. Mrs. Frederiksen was pacing the length of the kitchen, four steps back and four steps forth. After every five or six times, she would push open the plank door and peek out. The first ten times, there was nothing but the sound of rain. The eleventh time, there was a sound like the whole world was screaming.

Mrs. Frederiksen jerked the door shut and barred it. Then she hooked her arm through mine and pulled me back into her little bedroom, shouting at my sister to follow us. The grating shriek rose. The thick walls of the soddy couldn't do anything to soften it now.

I sank onto the bed when Mrs. Frederiksen pushed me down. My sister crouched on the floor, the lantern set beside her, her back against Mrs. Frederiksen's big train trunk. Her eyes were closed. Mrs. Frederiksen put her arm around my shoulders and held me tight against her as the wind smashed into the soddy, clawing, trying to get at us. I shouted to my sister, but my voice was silenced by the tearing roar of the wind. I reached out to take her hand, but she pulled it away. Then I closed my eyes, too.

CHAPTER TWO

✿ ✿ ✿

I will never forget the sound. If I live to be a hundred years old, I will remember it often, and it will take my breath away every time. It got so loud that I covered my ears with my hands and ducked my head for what felt like an eternity. I have no idea how Mrs. Frederiksen and I ended up on the floor, but we did, and she had pulled me into her lap, leaning me forward, covering me with her own body. And when the sound of the tornado stopped, the silence that replaced it was strange and liquid and it took a long time to seep into our ears.

"Are you all right?" I heard someone ask. The voice was muted, distant. It took me a moment more to realize that I still had my hands tight against my ears. I lowered them, staring at my fingers. They were shaking. I was shaking. My knees vibrated and my teeth chattered. Mrs. Frederiksen sat straighter and hugged me close, rocking back and forth, calming my shivers, slowing my heart. When she released me, I blinked and realized that my sister was silent, staring at the lantern. The flame had gone out. The wind had found it. I inhaled, then exhaled, then realized I could see my sister's face clearly. I looked up. The tornado had put a hole in the roof. I felt a spatter of rain on my cheek.

"Could have done without that," Mrs. Frederiksen said as we all got up and stood close together. She pulled Lib close, trying to hug her, but my sister stepped back.

"It probably stole my ladder, too," Mrs. Frederiksen said. "I just left it leaning against the soddy. Probably carried it off like a feather." Then she looked at me and I know we both had the same thought at the same instant. Never mind the ladder. The *chickens*. And then I thought about the horses and Bessie.

I turned, my legs still shaky. I felt Mrs. Frederiksen grip my shoulder. "Wait. The tornado's probably long gone," she said. "But let me look around."

I reached for Libby's hand, but she pulled free. I knew she was ashamed of being so scared and I also knew that she would never admit it, to me or to anyone else. Libby is tough. She has always taken care of us.

"Is it all right if I go outside?" I asked her, like I was three years old again. She didn't answer except to shoo me with her hands.

On my way through the kitchen, I saw that the wax-paper window was torn, and the place was gritty with dust. But nothing had been swept onto the floor or broken. Lib's bread dough had risen up out of the bowl—a big glob sagged from beneath the dampened tea towel onto the sideboard. Had we been in the bedroom that long? The fire was down to coals. It all seemed amazing to me—that the soddy was still standing, that the roaring wind had left anything behind. I wondered if the neighbors with planked houses had fared better or worse.

By the time I caught up, Mrs. Frederiksen was halfway to the barn. I could hear the horses blowing out long, frightened breaths, whinnying over and over. But there was no damage that I could see. When we opened the door, I sighed in relief. The roof was intact and the horses were scared, but not hurt. Bessie had a little bloody patch on her forehead—had she shoved at her gate trying to get out? Mrs. Frederiksen opened the grain bin.

The horses calmed almost instantly when they heard the lid creak. They loved the oats and cracked corn and they rarely got more than a little. Bessie bawled, clearly trying to make sure no one forgot that she was scared and needed comforting, too. For some reason, it struck me funny and I laughed aloud, then clapped a hand over my mouth, afraid Mrs. Frederiksen would scold me. But she was smiling, too. But then we both knew it was time to go check the chickens and our smiles faded.

As we walked back up to the house, Mrs. Frederiksen took my hand and held it tight as we rounded the corner. The chickens lay scattered inside the coop. All but three of them were dead, and those three were half plucked by the wind. I hadn't once thought about bringing them inside. I had been too afraid. I didn't realize I was crying until Mrs. Frederiksen wiped my cheek and bent down to look into my eyes. "This is my fault," she said quietly. "Not yours. I have seen tornadoes before and I should have thought to bring them inside. I was just plain scared and I forgot."

I swallowed and blinked back my tears—it eased my heart a little to hear her say that. "Margret?" Mrs. Frederiksen put her hand on my shoulder. "Will you just go in and make sure your sister is all right? I'll get started here. We'll clean up the place a bit, then see what all needs doing before nightfall."

Inside, Libby had already wiped the sideboard clean. Now she was pounding the bread dough, forcing it back to half its risen size. The main thing was to keep the yeast alive, I knew. Mrs. Procket, back in Iowa, had taught us that. We had stayed with her family for only two months, but she had taught us both to cook. Libby had been an excellent student, and was a grand cook now. Her bread was perfect, every time. I knew that if the yeast died, we'd have to go neighbor-begging to get a cup of starter—and that it might not be as good as the one Lib had now.

I found the broom and began sweeping the bits of dirt and grass the wind had torn loose. Libby seemed fine. I knew better than to ask her. But her cheeks were pink again, a good sign. "Will the dough be all right?" I asked when she glanced up.

She nodded. "It's still warm. Barely."

"That's good," I said, just to say something. Libby's lips were tight, her words barely escaping.

"All the chickens dead?" she asked.

I nodded, still feeling half sick. "All but three."

Libby shook her head. "She should have brought them in."

I looked at my sister. "That's what she said, Lib. She feels terrible. So do I. I should have—"

"You think she's just perfect, don't you?"

I blinked. "No. But I like her."

Libby nodded. "Remember the Baxters?"

I blinked again and nodded. The Baxters had owned a little dry-goods store in Kansas City. Mrs. Baxter had set us to work sweeping, sorting buttons, polishing brass buckles, and whatever else two girls could do. She had seemed very nice, but then one day she had slapped me, right across the face, for accidentally getting in her way. Lib had gotten me up in the dark that very night, and we had left at a run.

"If you know people long enough," Libby whispered, "they show their true colors. Mrs. Frederiksen is not family to us. Don't forget that."

Libby had a stone-hard look on her face I knew all too well. And she was right about some of the people we had stayed with, but not all of them. I could tell about Mrs. Frederiksen. She had a kind heart.

I finished sweeping and then stood staring up at the hole in the sod roof in Mrs. Frederiksen's little bedchamber for a few minutes. I could hear Libby banging around in the kitchen, but I just held still and refused to think about anything. I had had lots of practice at it, staying with people we barely knew, walking all night to get to another farm, or days and days and days to get to the next town, being scared half the time. When I was little, Libby had carried me.

I stared at the patch of sky and told myself everything was going to be all right. It was sort of like I was pinning my worried thoughts down, stilling them. Once they were quiet, I went back outside.

Using the corner of the little porch as a table, Mrs. Frederiksen had skinned the chickens to avoid the mess of plucking what remained of their feathers. Now she was dressing them out, her gutting knife in her right hand. When she saw me she made a gesture that told me it was all right if I didn't want to help. But I couldn't see why the worst chore should be hers alone. I should have thought of the chickens, too—I was the one who gathered eggs almost every day.

I took a deep breath and pitched in. It was terrible. But it would be worse if we wasted the meat. So I fetched water so Mrs. Frederiksen could rinse the carcasses as she went. Then I buried the offal while Mrs. Frederiksen did the butchering. And when she was done, we carried the meat into the house.

Libby looked up sharply and made a little sound of dismay. There was no chance of her special

Independence Day supper now. I wasn't sure whether she was angry about that, or just didn't want the extra cooking, or if the sight of the poor chickens upset her. She turned to stoke the fire as Mrs. Frederiksen and I laid the meat on one end of the sideboard and washed up.

Then Libby made another faint little sound, an odd one I hadn't heard her make before. I was about to say something when it came again, barely audible, and I realized Libby had not made it. It was coming from outside.

"Shall we just bake it all? Or make a stew as well?" Mrs. Frederiksen asked. And Libby answered but I didn't really hear what she said. The little sound came once more.

Mrs. Frederiksen was talking to Libby—I was the one nearest the door—and I could tell neither of them had heard anything. I am not sure why I didn't say something. Maybe I could tell that there was no danger in whatever creature had made the sad little sound. Or maybe I was just so happy to see Mrs. Frederiksen talking to Libby—and Libby answering back in a civil voice—that I didn't want to interrupt them.

Whatever the reason, I went out the door by myself and neither one of them called me back. I walked out into the yard and glanced up at the sky.

The clouds were thinning. They were more light gray than black now. And the wind was still. I lowered my eyes and scanned the yard, then looked down the path.

There was a horse I had never seen before standing down by the barn. As I started down the path, he jerked his head up and stared at me. He was a tall, jet-black gelding, fine-boned and handsome, a well-bred saddle horse. But his eyes were wild with fear. I stopped, afraid he would gallop away. But he didn't. I counted to thirty, then started toward him again, taking small steps, holding my breath, hoping he wouldn't run. As I got closer I could see why he hadn't.

CHAPTER THREE

❦ ❦ ❦

*T*he horse was hurt bad. At first, all I could think to do was get him inside, confined in a stall, so that he wouldn't try to gallop—or even walk. I wanted to bind the wound with rags, stop the blood that was running down his left foreleg. But with every slow, careful step I took toward him, I knew that it might be impossible to help. He was scared, trembling from fear and pain—and probably cold. He was soaked from the rain. A little wind was coming up from the west. I saw him shudder. How could I lead him to the barn? There wasn't a bit of tack on him—not even a halter.

I stopped on the path when I heard Mrs. Frederiksen calling me. I didn't want her to come. Not now. Two strangers would almost certainly scare the gelding into trying to run. I half turned and tipped my head in the direction of the horse.

"I see," she called quietly. "I'll go back in and leave the door open. Shout if you need help."

I didn't turn or even lift my hand to let her know I had heard. I was afraid to. The gelding was tossing his head now, clearly uneasy. He took a step away from me, and I winced when I saw how badly he was limping.

"It's all right," I said quietly. "Please just trust me. I know you don't know me and I know you are scared, but if you trust me, I promise to take care of you and Mrs. Frederiksen will help me find out where you belong."

He lowered his head a little and flared his nostrils, blowing out a long, fluttering breath. I wasn't sure what it meant, so I just stood still. After a few minutes had passed, he snorted and shook his mane, then lowered his head again. Bennie and Tish must have heard him because they both whickered long and low, asking what stranger was so close to their barn.

Slowly, I backed up the path, almost to the soddy, then I started toward the barn again, taking a long arcing route off the path that took me farther away from the horse until I was well past him. Then I turned and walked straight back toward the barn door, where he couldn't see me anyway. Once I was out of his sight, I hurried. Bennie and Tish were finished with their oats and seemed grateful to be led out to their pasture. I took Bennie first. Once he was settled and grazing on the rain-wet grass, I started back for Tish.

The whole time I was glancing at the black gelding. He limped forward, angling toward the pasture fence but away from me. Bennie met him at the railing and they exchanged long whuffling breaths the way horses do when they are strangers. When I brought Tish out, I let her walk a step or two, then I stopped her. Then two more and a pause. Bennie did what he always did. He came to the gate to wait for her. I held my breath again, hoping. The black horse followed Bennie, keeping as close as he could, considering the fence between them.

I walked Tish slowly, keeping her between me and the black as we got to the pasture. I leaned beneath her neck to slide the rails, then stepped back. I then stood stock-still as Tish stepped forward, nudging Bennie a little as she went in, to make him let her pass. I felt my heart lift as the black gelding followed close behind her, entering the pasture quietly. Once he was inside, I closed the gate, then ran for the house.

"The bleeding is bad?" Mrs. Frederiksen asked, opening the bottom drawer in her little wooden dresser. I saw a stack of neatly folded rags—faded, soft cloth from worn clothing and bedding. She handed me the whole stack.

I nodded. "It's going down his leg. I couldn't really see the cut—I didn't get close enough. But he's limping pretty bad and the bleeding—"

She nodded and held up one hand. "We should get him into a stall. Do you want me to try to approach him?"

I shook my head.

"You be very careful. Don't loop the lead around your hand, drop it and get back if he seems too fear-wild to handle. Remember—he didn't have a bedroom to hide in and no one was there to tell him it would pass. He has to be scared to death it'll come back."

I nodded. "I'll be careful. Once I have him in a stall, I'll come get you."

She smiled. "Shout if you need me before that."

"Stay here, Margret," Libby said. Then she turned to Mrs. Frederiksen, and I could see a stony look on my sister's face that I knew all too well. When she thought she was protecting me, she didn't care at all for politeness or anything else.

"You want my eleven-year-old sister to risk getting hurt," Lib said evenly, staring at Mrs.

Fredricksen, "so that you can sell the horse or keep it, or whatever you decide to—"

"I won't get hurt. He's not mean, he's just scared," I interrupted her.

Mrs. Frederiksen squared her shoulders. I had never seen her look angry, but she looked furious now. Still, her voice was low and calm. "The horse is injured," she told Lib. "Margret says it doesn't seem vicious and she is better with horses than the two of us combined times ten. Do you disagree with that?"

Libby's face had truly turned to stone. She didn't answer.

"Do you think that we should simply let it bleed to death if it is in our power to help it?"

Libby's eyes flashed. "Ask the chickens."

I saw Mrs. Frederiksen's face change from anger to hurt. Libby must have seen it, too, because she looked satisfied. I hated her when she got like this. Mrs. Fredericksen hadn't done anything wrong.

"Libby, that's not fair," I began, but Mrs. Frederiksen held up one hand to quiet me.

"Do you want to try to help the horse?" she asked me. I nodded. "Then go. Be very careful. Take no chances at all even if it means the horse dies. Do you hear?"

"Yes, ma'am," I said, then turned to go out the door before Libby could say anything more. I ran to the barn first and opened one of the unused stalls. I pitched in straw bedding, then filled a water bucket and the hayrick. I left the rags on the clean bedding, grabbed a bucket of grain, then ran back to the pasture.

The bleeding had slowed, but it hadn't stopped. It took a long time and half the bucket of grain to get close enough to slide a halter over his ears. Once it was on, he let me lead him back toward the gate, slowly, a step or two at a time.

Tish and Bennie wanted to come, too, and for a long moment, I was afraid the black would shy away because they crowded him so. I stopped near the gate and let them finish the grain, feeding the black's share to him from the palm of my hand. Then, when Bennie and Tish realized it was gone and went back to grazing, I led the gelding back out of the pasture.

He followed me willingly a few steps, then he stopped, trembling, holding his head so high that he pulled my arm nearly straight up in the air. I stood with him, waiting. I couldn't see what scared him and maybe I would never figure it out. But if I tried to bully him into going toward the barn, I knew I would lose. And so would he.

I glanced at his leg and winced. The cut was deep and walking had freshened the bleeding. Even if it healed perfectly, it would leave a terrible scar. And if it soured, he would probably die. "Please," I said quietly, rubbing his shoulder. He shook his mane, but his head stayed high and I knew he wouldn't let me pull him forward yet—so I didn't try.

I wondered who he belonged to. No one too near, I was pretty sure. There were only a few farms between us and the Platte River and we had come here from the northeast. I would have noticed a horse as tall and graceful as he was if I had seen him in someone's pasture. Libby and I had come across this stretch of prairie slowly with the Gleason family, walking behind their wagon, the oxen plodding along. Most of the horses here were like Bennie and Tish—heavy-bodied and strong, good for pulling the wagon and for plowing and cutting sod. But even the few saddle horses weren't anything like this one. I rested my hand on the gelding's neck and he calmed some, but I was still wary of trying to make him walk, so I just waited, both of us staring past the barn, at the horizon.

"Where do you live?" I asked him. "Not close, I don't think. How did you get here?"

He lifted his head, then lowered it again. He seemed to like being talked to, so I told him how

Lib and I had come west without really meaning to. For nine years, we had mostly walked a day or two, then worked a day or two for a few decent suppers, then walked again.

"If we said we were orphans," I told the gelding, "most people wanted to help us, because they were good-hearted," I explained. It was true. For a long time, when Libby had wanted to move on, there was an argument with whoever we were staying with at the time about how dangerous it was for two girls to travel alone. So Lib had started lying somewhere along the way. She told people we had gotten separated from our folks and that we were on our way to meet them in whatever town we were east of at the time. Sometimes, listening to her, it sounded so real that I pretended it was true.

The black gelding shook his mane. "But if I had ever seen you, I'd have noticed you," I said, just to keep talking as I tugged the halter gently. He took two steps, then stopped and lowered his head. He set about smelling me up and down, nibbling at my hair. I held still even though his breath tickled my cheeks and the back of my neck. The bleeding had slowed again and I wanted to get it stopped—which meant he had to trust me. When he was finished smelling me, he lifted his head again and looked at the barn. It was time. I tugged gently at the halter and he came forward. We stopped twice on the way to let him gather his courage and to rest his leg. Then he followed me through the doors and down the wide aisle to the stall I had gotten ready for him.

He went straight in, so he was probably used to stalls. He plunged his muzzle into the water bucket and drank deep, then looked at me, his chin dripping.

"I need to bind that cut," I said. "The bleeding has slowed, but if you get grass stuck in it, or dirt, the wound could sour . . ."

He shuffled and shook his mane.

I thought about getting a rope to tether him. I knew that was what most people would do. But I had a feeling that he would get scared again if I did that. It seemed like I had his trust and I didn't want to lose it. If I did, there would be no way to help him. So I just went through the rags and picked out the longest one, then tore it in half lengthwise to make a few yards of bandage. I saw the gelding shift his weight, ready to back away.

"Stand still," I pleaded with him in a low, gentle voice. "Just let me get it done and then you can have more grain and some hay and sleep awhile. Just stand still."

It was like I had spoken in horse language and he had understood. He lowered his head and stood without moving as I gently pressed the wound closed, then wrapped it with the cloth just tight enough to make the blood stop altogether. Then I rubbed his ears and dried his coat with feed sacks. And all the while I praised his patience and his bravery and thanked him over and over for trusting me.

"How did you get hurt?" I asked him. "Was it something the wind picked up and flung through the air?" I shivered, remembering the sound.

He rubbed his cheek against my shoulder so hard that I had to brace myself against the railings to keep from falling over. I looked at the bandage. The blood had seeped into the tightly wrapped cloth, but just barely.

"I'm going to go tell Mrs. Frederiksen that you are all right," I said.

He leaned forward and smelled my face, and my hair, then went back to the grain bucket.

I went out and closed his stall, so relieved that I was grinning at nothing. Then, when I went out the barn door, I nearly bumped into Libby.

"I heard you talking," she said. "Mrs. Frederiksen said we should leave you alone, but I came to check and make sure . . ." She trailed off, looking past me at the gelding standing calmly in the stall. "Does he appreciate your tender nursing?"

Her voice was hard, mocking. So I didn't answer her.

"Margret," she said suddenly. "I'm not sure how much longer I can stand that prying old woman. She asked me just now about our parents. Why would she think that is any of her business?"

I shook my head. "She likes us, Libby," I said. "She probably feels a little sorry for us and—"

"We don't need her pity," Libby said. "And it isn't her concern—"

"Maybe not," I interrupted her, getting angry. "But it's mine. And you won't tell me anything about them, either."

I felt terrible the instant the words left my mouth because Libby's face just collapsed and her eyes filled with tears. I apologized and I held her hands as long as she would let me. Then she stepped back.

"I just can't talk about it," she whispered. And I didn't say a single mean word back to her, because I could see how it hurt her to even say that much.

CHAPTER FOUR
❦ ❦ ❦

The next day the black gelding was calmer and he ate all the grain I gave him. The day after that, I changed his bandage and washed the soiled one in soap and hot water, then hung it on the line to dry and walked back down to the barn. Once I was sure that the new bandage was tight—but not too tight—I led Bennie and Tish out to the pasture, then the gelding. He stood at the gate after I slid the rails back in place. I rubbed his forehead and stroked his neck.

"You are a good, sweet horse," I told him. "And it'll break my heart, but someone will come looking for you soon."

He shook his mane, like he had understood but was disagreeing with me. That made me laugh a little—but I had meant what I said. A horse this good would be important to whoever owned him. Someone would come. I only wished it would take a few weeks, not a few days. This might very well be as close as I would ever come to having a horse of my own and I never wanted it to end.

Libby was sweeping the porch when I walked back up.

"You going to spend half of every single day down at the barn?" she asked me. "What about your work?"

"She did most of her chores early," Mrs. Frederiksen said from the doorway, startling us both. It was true. I had carried in water and firewood before it had gotten light. I had milked Bessie and cooled the milk, thrown out the sour curds for the chickens to eat, and started the next batch. And I had already swept the porch, too, though the grit the tornado had drilled into the cracks between the planks would probably take a hundred sweepings to get rid of.

Mrs. Frederiksen had the egg basket in one hand. It was empty. She lifted it and shook her head. "We can't expect the poor half-bald things to go right back to laying after being so terrified, I guess," she said, then sighed. "Maybe we will have to drive the team into Littleton one day soon, see if anyone has pullets for sale."

Libby went back to her work without saying a word. I looked at Mrs. Frederiksen. "Do you know anyone around here who might have hens? I could ride Tish."

Mrs. Frederiksen shrugged. "I barely see my neighbors anymore. But someone at the Harvest Day get-together will know."

Libby turned around. "Harvest Day?"

Mrs. Frederiksen nodded. "It started when this was all wheat and corn country. After the harvest, we would take a day off, play games, dance half the night. Now more and more are raising cattle, but we still get together. Every year, after the bigger ranches get their hay in, the women get organized and start cooking and the musicians limber up their bows."

"When?" I asked her.

"The last week in August."

"What day is this?" I asked her.

"Laundry day," Libby said.

I glared at her. "I mean the date. July sixth?"

Mrs. Frederiksen nodded. "The sixth, yes. Why? Do you like to dance?"

"No," Libby said flatly. "She has no idea how to dance. She's thinking that someone out there will probably know where that gelding belongs."

Mrs. Frederiksen was looking at me, not Libby, and I am sure she saw the expression on my face when Libby was unkind enough to announce the truth. From the instant Mrs. Frederiksen had mentioned Harvest Day, that had been my first thought. Even if no one came to the soddy before then, we would be honor bound to ask people at the dance. And someone there would probably know.

"Well," Mrs. Frederiksen said carefully, "you may be right, Libby. But that is almost six weeks off and Margret can be that poor horse's angel until then." She looked at me like a person who has done something mean and they want you to forgive them. She hadn't done anything at all, but I smiled anyway so she would know that I didn't hold her to account for the simple truth.

"How much would a horse like that gelding cost?" I asked, without knowing I was going to.

Mrs. Frederiksen sighed and shrugged. "I honestly don't know, dearie."

"More than you will ever have in your life," Libby said. "Would you build up the fire a little, Margret?"

So I stoked the fire; then, without looking at Mrs. Frederiksen or Libby, I went back out the door and down the path to the pasture. The black gelding saw me coming and he lifted his head and nickered. I watched him walk toward me. He was still favoring his wounded leg, of course, but it seemed a little less than the day before. Maybe having the bandage kept the pain down. He was so happy to see me that my heart lifted a little.

"I can't stay too long," I told him when he got to the fence and reached over the top rail to nibble at my hair. "Today is laundry day."

He stared off toward the northwest while I rubbed his forehead. "Is that where you're supposed to be? Somewhere between here and Denver City?" Or maybe, I thought, he had come from a lot farther north, from Fort Collins or Fort Laramie—maybe some army officer was missing his favorite horse.

But it seemed most likely that the black belonged to someone in Littleton. We had only seen the main street twice, going in with Mrs. Frederiksen for flour from the Rough and Ready Mill and cloth for aprons from the little dry-goods outfit. The first time we had gone, she had bought us each a good dress, and an extra blanket each. Libby wouldn't let me wear the dress. Maybe she was saving them for when we moved on, to help us look nice for the next place.

It was odd. Some people were more likely to take us in if we looked ragged. Others liked us better if we had good clothes. Mrs. Gleason had insisted we travel with them because we looked so tattered, I think. We had come the last forty miles here walking behind the Gleasons' wagon. They hoped to buy a ranch somewhere farther south, along the South Platte River, and raise cattle. The Gleasons had been very nice to us. I wondered if they had found their place yet. I wondered if we would ever see them again. They had two sons—cute, mischievous boys. And I know Mrs. Gleason would have tried to get us to stay with them.

But Libby wasn't stupid. Not ever. She had waited until we were seeing more farms, more little sod houses and some bigger planked ones each day, before she had decided we had to go off on our own again. She said that the Gleasons would expect dawn-to-dusk hard work out of us if they were going to be building a homestead—and they would likely tell us to move on once most of the hard work was done.

Maybe she was right. But we would never know. Libby made the decision, and we had left when everyone else was asleep, at the height of a full moon, like we always did, trudging along under the stars.

We would end up in Denver City for a while, once we moved on, I was sure. Libby liked living in towns. I didn't. I liked farmwork much better than sweeping sidewalks and begging shopkeepers to trade us food for stacking cartons or putting buttons in boxes or whatever tedious task they had. I sighed. If we ended up in Denver City, Libby was right about not being able to take care of a horse. But if we stayed here with Mrs. Frederiksen, she was wrong.

That thought made me catch my breath for an instant. If no one came to claim the gelding, and if I could convince Libby to stay here, and if Mrs. Frederiksen wouldn't mind . . .

I knew that was too many *ifs*, but it made me smile. I liked Mrs. Frederiksen more all the time. And if the beautiful black gelding could really be mine . . .

I reined in my thoughts and marched back up the path. The only way Libby would consider staying was if nothing went wrong. So I got to work. I did every single ding-dang chore I could think of and then nearly broke my back at the washboard. I strung up the second clothesline rope and carried the basket of wet bed linens out. I noticed Libby glancing at me, but I refused to look back.

I didn't go down to the barn again until evening, to bring the horses in, then feed and milk. I changed the black gelding's bandage, too. I stayed in his stall and just stood with him for a long while once I was finished, letting him nibble at my hair. He seemed so happy to have company, so grateful for kind attention. I knew the tornado had to have terrified him. He had been hurt, lost, and scared when I had found him. But he hadn't trusted me at first. And that made me wonder if he was used to kindness, or if he had been expecting something else.

"I wish you could talk," I told him as I forced myself to open his stall gate and go out. He whickered at me. I knew he couldn't really understand me, but it was remarkable how often it seemed like he did.

The next day I worked so hard that I was done with most everything by noon. Then I helped Mrs. Frederiksen look for her ladder so we could fix the roof. She had been right. The tornado had picked it up and carried it off. In the end, Libby helped, and we all three walked a mile or two apiece, back and forth across the grass, looking until it got dark. The ladder was gone all the way to who-knows-where.

A few days later, over our evening plate of beans and rice, Mrs. Frederiksen decided that we would look no more, we would make another ladder. That meant we would have to find three slim, straight sapling trees, probably pines of one kind or another. She had more of the rawhide, saved from the last steer she had raised, already cut into inch-wide strips. She filled a bucket and soaked a dozen or so. All of that took less than five minutes. It was the wood that was hard to find. We could have cut limbs from her elm trees, but they weren't all that big yet, and she hated to set them back.

So Mrs. Frederiksen and I went all the way to the South Platte River to find saplings, driving Tish and Bennie on the wagon road for five or six miles. We passed three farms, one a pretty place with trees planted along the fence lines, then we cut across the prairie grass at a slow clip-clopping walk, veering around the clumps of buffalo grass. Once we were close to the river, we heard a long whistle and Mrs. Frederiksen reined in so we could watch the Colorado & Southern train go past on the other side of the river.

"Statehood is coming soon," Mrs. Frederiksen said as we stared as the huge engine chugging along, clouds of smoke billowing out of its smokestack. "Colleen said people are coming into Denver all the time now. Even Littleton is growing—and not just gold miners who decided to stay after they went bust. People are coming here to live."

I glanced at her and saw that her eyes were teary. Was she thinking about her husband or her sons not being here to see the Colorado Territory become a state? I envied her in a strange way. I knew I should feel sad about my parents, but when I tried to, there wasn't anything inside me but an empty place. I envied Libby, too. At least she could miss them. All I could do was wonder what it was like to have parents, wonder what mine had been like, wonder if I would ever know. Mrs. Frederiksen reached out and took my hand and squeezed it, like she had understood my thoughts. Then she clucked at Bennie and Tish and we went on.

Mrs. Frederiksen had a hatchet, and like most of the farm women I had known in my life, she was handy with it. Chopping down three saplings took very little time. It took us longer to clean off the branches and figure out how to lay them across the wagon bed so the ends wouldn't drag on the ground. Longest of all was getting there and back.

The prairie looks flat, but it isn't. There are clumps of tangled grass and grass-covered rocks for the big wooden wagon wheels to go up over and there are prairie dog and gopher burrows that collapse under the weight of a wagon. It was just plain painful, the wagon falling and rising, jolting along. And the driver's bench was a bare birch plank. My backside was aching by the time we got home.

The next day, Libby took kitchen duty as usual—she was the best cook out of the three of us, Mrs. Frederiksen said—and it was her preference anyway. I milked, fed the horses and Bessie, then carried the milk to the house. I strained the whey out of the next batch of curds. Libby was pouring it into her bread batter as I went back out.

Then I helped Mrs. Frederiksen and learned how to make a ladder. She wrapped the rawhide strips in tight figure eights to hold the crosspieces to the vertical rails. Then she looked up. "Watch," she said, then pulled the ends of the soaked rawhide back beneath itself with a little metal hook she had made from a bucket bale. I nodded. It was clever. The rawhide would shrink as it dried, so the loose ends would be held fast. She made sure the ladder rungs were level, then leaned it against the house to let the rawhide dry.

"You know a lot of good things," I told her, then blushed. It sounded silly, like something a three-year-old would say. But she only smiled.

"I know this much," she said. "You are a very good person, Margret. I think you ought to work in the barn all day tomorrow. As soon as the chores are finished, you could walk the gelding around, get him a little exercise. We can fix the roof the next day. It isn't going to rain."

I hugged her, then stepped back when I heard the soddy door open. But Libby hadn't seen the hug, I could tell. She wasn't frowning. I sighed. Libby never liked it when I got too attached to the people we stayed with. She didn't want me arguing when she decided it was time to go—especially when I was little. Once, my crying had wakened the farmwife and there had been an awful row, with arguing and anger all the way till morning. I had been four or five and they had a dog I had come to love. Chester. I couldn't picture his owners, but I remembered him, perfectly.

The next morning, the chickens laid three eggs. Libby made breakfast while I milked and carried wood and water. When we had finished eating, I left without telling Libby I would be with the horses most of the day. She wouldn't miss me for a few hours anyway, she was used to me being gone that long to get my chores done.

It was a glorious morning. The sun was warm and the air was soft and sweet. I went into the barn and changed the gelding's bandage, then walked the horses out to the pasture one by one. The gelding was happy to be out of his stall, and when I put him in the pasture, he tossed his head and switched his tail a little before he dropped his head to graze. He was feeling better.

I mucked out the stalls. It was one of the chores that hurt Mrs. Frederiksen's back, so I felt good keeping her from having to do it. And I had liked being in the barn with Tish and Bennie from the start, long before I had found the gelding. Now, I was happier here than anywhere else—and today, as soon as I got the chores done, I would get to take the gelding for a walk.

As I rolled the wooden barrow back and forth to the offal heap, Bessie ate her grain. When she was finished, she bawled at me and pushed against her stall gate. She knew where the horses had gone and was reminding me that she had a right to graze, too. I slipped a leather lead around her neck and walked her out. Or, really, she walked *me*. She knew the way perfectly well and was in a hurry to get there.

The black gelding was at the far end of the pasture. When I slid the rails back so Bessie could go in, he noticed me and lifted his head and whickered. Then he walked toward me. He was still favoring his leg, but it seemed a little better. His held his head high and arched his tail—and he looked like no other horse I had ever seen in my life. I laid one hand flat on his shoulder, looking at the bandage. It was clean. The cut had stopped seeping.

"You know who he looks like?" I heard Mrs. Frederiksen call.

I looked up to see her smiling at me, walking down the path. She had a lovely expression on her face and I could tell what a beauty she had been as a girl.

"Who does he look like?" I called back.

"A man I once loved," she said when she got closer. "Years before I met my William." I could see sadness in her eyes. "Flynn was the handsomest Irishman who ever lived, so far as I know. He loved to sing, to make people happy. But he went off to the war and he never came back to me." She stopped by the railing. I didn't ask her what war, or if he had intended to marry her, or anything else because I hate it when people ask me about my parents. I turned to the gelding as Mrs. Frederiksen came close to pat his forehead.

"Mr. Flynn? Is that who you look like?" I said, shaking my finger at him.

The gelding tossed his mane, his neck arched.

Mrs. Frederiksen laughed softly and I glanced at her. "See that? He's flattered, as well he should be. Padraic Flynn was wonderful. The world is poorer without him." She reached over the top rail to pat the gelding again. He backed away, then hesitated, turning to look at me like a child would, asking permission. I nudged him forward.

"He takes your advice," she said, rubbing his forehead. Then she looked at me. "He knows a good heart when he meets one."

I blushed. Sometimes the things she said made me feel wonderful in a way I couldn't ever remember feeling in my whole life. I knew that Libby didn't trust anyone, ever, except me. And I knew that Mrs. Frederiksen wasn't family to us. But she was kind and honest and I was almost certain she would never do anything to hurt me or Libby. She wouldn't. I felt it in my heart.

CHAPTER FIVE

❧ ❧ ❧

I kept walking the gelding, almost every day. He was still limping, but it seemed a little less with every day that passed. One morning, Mrs. Frederiksen came down to the pasture gate to see how he was doing. We were watching him graze when we heard the sound of hoofbeats.

We walked up the little rise side by side, then stood in the stand of elms, looking east through the branches. There were three riders galloping up the road. They wore hats like cowhands.

"Do you know them?" I asked her.

She shook her head. "I don't think so." Then she reached out and took my hand for a second, squeezing tight. "I have an intuition about this, Margret. Put Mr. Flynn in the barn, will you please? Hurry." She looked worried and I whirled around and ran down the hill.

I slowed near the pasture gate so I wouldn't spook the horses. I was scared. An intuition? Did she think one of the cowboys was the gelding's owner? Would she tell me to hide him if she thought that? Stealing a horse was a serious crime.

I approached the black, talking nonsense in the calmest voice I could manage, extending my hand slowly to grasp his halter. Once I had him, it was awkward, holding on to him and opening the gate, but I managed. I led him out and tried to put the rails back in place without letting go of his halter. I managed the middle one. Tish and Ben wouldn't try to jump it, I was sure.

I led the gelding at a trot to the barn. I gave him grain in his manger, then scattered a little more over his pile of dried grass. I didn't want him to start nickering to Bennie and Tish when he realized that I wasn't coming right back.

"Be good. Be quiet," I said, patting him before I closed his gate. I forced myself to walk calmly out of the barn, closed the door, then glanced up the hill. They weren't here yet. So I sprinted to shove the top and bottom rails back into place, then ran up the path.

They were getting close. I hesitated, then ran back downhill, bearing left, so that I passed between the pasture fence and the back of the house. Then I stopped to catch my breath before I walked at a normal pace to the chicken coop and went inside, hoping for at least one egg. The hoofbeats were loud now. The riders were nearly in the yard. I found two eggs and carried them palm up, forcing a half smile as I walked around the corner, trying to look like I had interrupted my chores to come see who was here.

Mrs. Frederiksen was already out on her little porch as the men reined in. I stared at them. One of them glanced at me as he dismounted and handed one of his companions his reins. He used one index finger to push his hat back so I could see his face. He was young and sort of handsome. And he seemed polite as he called out a good day to Mrs. Frederiksen. I turned to see her nod and blinked. She had a rifle in her right hand, the barrel slanting downward and to the side, half hidden by her full skirt. I hadn't known that she owned one. She held it with complete ease, loose and familiar, just like a man would. I had no doubt she was a crack shot and I could see the cowboy's face well enough to know the instant he noticed the gun. He stood up a little straighter.

I moved to lean against the soddy wall. They were cowboys, all of them, it looked like. Their clothing was rough and worn from endless riding. Both the men who hung back, waiting, sat astride sturdy, plain-looking horses. The riderless bay was finer-boned, much prettier. Maybe they were just wanting a drink of water or asking the way to Denver. Maybe they weren't looking for Flynn. I was too nervous then to notice the way Mrs. Frederiksen's name for the gelding had stuck in my thoughts, but I realized it later.

"It is a lovely day, isn't it, ma'am?" the cowboy said a second time.

This time Mrs. Frederiksen nodded, but she still didn't answer.

"Is your husband around?" he asked.

She nodded again and said nothing. I knew her well enough to know that she thought very little of liars and was trying to avoid it. Her William was around, in pure truth. He was buried up above the pasture. Mrs. Frederiksen was just being cautious. Why the cowboy would want to know could be as simple as wanting to get hired for a few days of work, or as wicked as wondering if there was a man around to protect an old woman and a girl. Two girls.

I could hear Libby banging pots in the kitchen. She was probably doing exactly what Mrs. Frederiksen was doing—being cautious. There was no way for the cowboy to know how many people were here. The kitchen noise could just as well have been made by two or three grown sons as one orphaned kitchen maid.

"Do you have business with my husband?" Mrs. Frederiksen asked abruptly.

The cowboy shrugged. "We were just wondering if you'd seen any horses running loose."

My heart stopped and I held my breath.

"My horses are in the pasture," she said.

Mrs. Frederiksen gestured and I saw the cowboy lean a little, to see past the elm trees. "But you haven't seen any horses besides your own?"

Mrs. Frederiksen tipped her head. "You lose a horse, mister?"

The cowboy nodded. "Four. And a few cattle. Did you see a tornado here?"

Mrs. Frederiksen nodded again. "We did. Terrible sound. Put a hole in my roof."

I waited for her to say more, but she didn't. Her face was stiff and stern, too, the exact opposite of her usual expression.

The cowboy took off his hat and worked the crown, shaping it with his fingers. "It came straight through our place, too."

Mrs. Frederiksen smiled a little. "Where's that? Nearby?"

An odd expression flickered across the cowboy's face and he gestured vaguely to the northeast.

I looked past him just as his horse sidled a little. The mare was a beautiful bay with a lovely face and an arch in her neck. I watched her move restlessly while the other two horses just lowered their heads and stood still. As she turned, the sunlight slanted across her coat and I noticed something else. Her flanks were covered with long whip welts.

"You saying you're from up north?" Mrs. Frederiksen asked after a long silence. "Do you know the McKenzies?"

The man nodded, but it was a second too late, like he'd had to decide whether or not to nod. In that instant I knew what Mrs. Frederiksen had known when she first saw them. These men weren't from around here. And now we both knew something else. They didn't seem honest. This one certainly wasn't. Or kind. I looked at the bay mare again and hated him for beating her.

"Come on, Eli," one of the other men said deliberately. He scratched his neck, then lifted his head and spoke in a stiff, careful voice. "Maybe we should be on our way."

"I'll be the one to decide that," the cowboy named Eli shouted back. The other man shrugged and didn't speak again.

"You hear anyone else talk about finding horses?" Eli asked Mrs. Frederiksen.

She shook her head and shifted the rifle in her hands.

"Well, then, thank you, ma'am," the cowboy said, smiling. He walked to his horse and mounted in one quick motion. He said something in a low, angry voice to the man who had called out to him. The man's face was stony and he said something back. They were arguing all the way down the path to the road, then instead of turning right and going on, they turned left.

Eli kicked his mare into a gallop and the others followed. He rode like he had been born in a saddle, and I winced as I saw him lashing the long end of his reins across his horse's flanks.

"Are they gone?" Libby asked in a low voice, without pushing the door open.

"Yes," I told her.

She came out onto the porch. "What happened?"

Mrs. Frederiksen looked at Libby for a long moment, then smiled. "Nothing, I hope. He said he had lost four horses and some cattle. I didn't tell him we had found one."

Libby's eyes widened. "Why?"

Mrs. Frederiksen glanced at me. "Because his mare had whip marks all over and he lied to me about where he's from. Mr. Flynn isn't our horse, but he doesn't belong to that cowboy, either." She took a long breath and I thought she was going to say more, but she shook her head and went inside.

"Mr. Flynn? You named him?" Libby demanded, the instant the door shut behind Mrs. Frederiksen.

I nodded, then shrugged. "She did. I like it."

"It's a silly name." Libby said. "What did the men say?"

I opened my mouth to explain just as the gelding whinnied from inside the barn. I turned, wondering if I should let him out, or wait awhile. When I glanced back, my sister was frowning.

"What happened, Margret? Did they say anything else?"

The gelding whinnied again and I turned to look past Lib, to the east. The men were tiny figures in the distance now and they were going straight back the way they had come.

"Margret!"

I looked back at my sister and repeated everything I could remember.

"And she just stood there holding the rifle?" Libby whispered.

I nodded.

Libby smiled—a thin little smile that meant she might not approve of something, but she admired it. "Mrs. Frederiksen is a tough old bird," she said. "But if they come back," Libby said quietly, "we'll leave. This is her fight, not ours. If it was up to me, we'd never have taken the horse in at all."

I blinked, startled by the finality in her voice. I am not sure why. I should have known. At the first sign of any kind of trouble, Libby had always wanted to leave. This time would be no different. It wouldn't matter to Libby if Mrs. Frederiksen was here all alone to face the cowboys when they came back. It wouldn't matter to her if the gelding ended up whipped bloody the first time the cowboy tried to force him to cross a river, or through a narrow gate, or any of the things that horses often shied at.

All Libby cared about was keeping us out of trouble. I knew it made sense, in a way, but it felt wrong this time. "I don't want to leave," I said, surprised by the sound of my own voice. I had thought it many times, but saying it aloud to my sister was another thing altogether.

"What?" Libby looked surprised, too.

"I like it here," I said quietly. "I like Mrs. Frederiksen a lot. And we shouldn't just leave her alone out here where—"

"She has a daughter in Denver," Libby interrupted in a hissy whisper. "A daughter who has so much money she doesn't know what to do with all of it. If Mrs. Frederiksen didn't want to live alone in this old soddy, she could have gone to Denver City long ago."

"She doesn't want to," I said. "She doesn't want to move into Denver." I glanced past Libby. The cowboys were nearly out of sight.

"We will leave here soon," Libby said sternly, like she was daring me to argue with her. "We need to get settled in somewhere for the winter."

I looked her in the eye. "It'd be wrong to leave Mrs. Frederiksen alone after the way she has helped us," I said as evenly as I could.

Libby opened her mouth to answer, then closed it. When she did speak, her voice was sharp, even though she kept it quiet so Mrs. Frederiksen wouldn't hear. "It isn't up to you where we stay. It's up to me. I have always been the one to decide and I still am. I've kept us safe so far."

I couldn't argue with that. "But I don't want to go, Libby," I whispered.

"Mrs. Frederiksen is a nice enough old woman," she said in a low voice. "But she is not family. We are all we have. The two of us. Don't forget that, Margret. Ever."

The gelding neighed again and I spun around and ran all the way down to the barn. I burst through the doors and ran to stand in front of his stall, trying to calm myself so I wouldn't scare him. But I couldn't. Tears were rolling down my cheeks.

I closed my eyes and felt warm grass-scented breath on my cheek. Flynn nudged my shoulder. I rubbed his forehead without opening my eyes. We stood like that for a long time. He loved being petted, and every second I stood there, I felt a little better, a little stronger. Libby had always made all our decisions, but maybe it was time for things to change. I wasn't a baby anymore. For an instant, thinking that made me feel grown up. Then I shivered. If I refused to go, would she leave without me?

CHAPTER SIX

❧ ❧ ❧

*T*he summer days slid past. One week, then two went by and July was nearly gone. At first, I looked eastward twenty times a day, afraid I would see the cowboys riding back, but they didn't come. I led the gelding around almost every day. His wound slowly closed and each day he favored the leg a little less. Then, finally, the limp was gone. Mrs. Frederiksen had me rub honey into the puckering scar and it wasn't nearly as bad as I thought it was going to be.

Flynn was calm and sweet. I got in the habit of walking down to the barn at sunset and giving him a little grain to eat. I loved talking to him, and he seemed to listen. He loved being patted and fussed over. One cool evening, on a whim, I climbed up on the stall rails and gently eased my weight onto his back, swinging one leg over, then slowly sitting upright. He didn't seem to mind. So I got on him most evenings after that. Sometimes I daydreamed about riding him, galloping along the road like an autumn wind. But mostly I just sat on his back, braiding and unbraiding his mane while I told him . . . everything.

I talked about Libby a lot. She was too quiet lately and I knew she was thinking about leaving. One evening, I started trying to remember everywhere we had ever lived and I couldn't. But as I went backward through all the couples, all the families, all the places, I realized Libby had two reasons for leaving. Either someone had treated us badly—which made sense—or I was starting to make a friend—animal or human.

Thinking that made me so uneasy I slid off the gelding's back and went out of the barn, walking away from the soddy for a little ways before I stopped and sat in the grass, staring out at the silhouettes of the distant trees that lined the South Platte, and the last of the orange-red sunset. I let out a long breath. Libby loved me and I loved her. But I was tired of moving and I *did* like it right here, with Mrs. Frederiksen. It was like having a kind grandmother, except she was more interesting than any grandmother I had ever met.

She had never once reminded us that she had taken us in, had never once made us feel unwelcome, not even when Libby was crabby. Mrs. Frederiksen shared the eggs equally and didn't say a word about having to do it. And unless someone claimed him, I knew she would let me keep Flynn.

I rocked back and forth, thinking, finally admitting it to myself. If it were up to me I would stay right here as long as I possibly could. Flynn whickered from inside the barn and I stood up and walked back, grateful to be distracted from my circling thoughts.

Things were all right for the next few days and August came in with three or four days so hot I could barely walk barefoot on the path to the barn. In the afternoons, clouds piled up and thunder rolled down the valley, but it didn't rain. Flynn was nervous and I spent hours in the barn, sitting on his back and talking to him, making sure he didn't get scared and hurt himself trying to get out of the stall.

Then, one evening, when Libby was inside making supper, I walked out to the garden and asked Mrs. Frederiksen if it was all right with her if I rode Flynn.

She nodded her head. "I can't see why not. He's sound—he canters on his own in the pasture.

So long as you stay on this side of the river and more or less in sight of the house, I won't worry. Maybe you should lead him first, though, and ride Tish. Still it's a risk," she added, and I knew what she meant.

"I thought of that," I admitted. "But he isn't from right around here or someone would have gone from one place to the next looking for him."

"You're probably right," she said. "But there is no way to know."

I nodded. But whoever owned Flynn would find him sooner or later anyway. Harvest Day was only a few weeks off now. After that, I might never get a chance to ride him.

"Maybe Libby could ride Tish and you could ride Flynn?" Mrs. Frederiksen asked.

I shook my head. "She's afraid of horses. She never rides."

Mrs. Frederiksen arched her brows. "Oh. Well, then maybe tomorrow before you go riding, you two could plan a picnic," she said as she slid the bar across to hold the barn doors closed. "Just the two of you, just for fun."

I stared at her a moment. Is that what girls with parents would do? Plan picnics that were just for fun? "We've never done anything like that," I said.

She put her arm around my shoulders as we started up the path. "You are welcome to stay here as long as you wish," she said, as though we had been talking about that, not picnics. "Both of you."

"Maaaarrrrgret!" Libby yelled from the porch. This time I called back, realizing she couldn't see us in the gathering dusk. She didn't answer, but she went back inside. When we got there, she had supper ready. I made a fuss over her dumplings and she seemed startled, then pleased.

Mrs. Frederiksen smiled. "Mine are always heavy as mud," she said, shaking her head. "You should teach Margret how to make them. I have receipts from my sisters. They are precious to me."

I looked at her. "Where are your sisters? Do they live in Denver?"

She sighed. "One in San Francisco, and one back east in the United States—in Virginia. Oh, how I miss them. We write letters a few times a year." She looked at me, then Libby, then back. "You are very lucky to have each other."

I nodded. Libby glanced at me and I smiled at her and she smiled back.

The next day, I made a point of bringing in extra firewood and water before I told Libby that I was going to take Tish and Flynn out for a canter if she didn't need my help for a while.

"You're riding Tish?" she asked sharply.

I nodded. "And leading the gelding. I will stay on this side of the river and mostly in sight of the soddy."

Libby shook her head. "What if those cowboys come back?"

I had no idea what to say to that and I was glad when I heard Mrs. Frederiksen's footsteps on the porch. Libby explained that I wanted to ride, then repeated her question. I knew she was hoping that Mrs. Frederiksen would forbid me to go. But she didn't.

"Libby, I've thought about it long and hard and I don't think those cowboys will ever come back here."

Libby's frowned. "Why?"

Mrs. Frederiksen faced her. "He lied about being from around here. I could tell that plain as day. And he never described the horses or the cows." She glanced at me, then looked at Libby again. "Perhaps he was just hoping to claim anyone's stock that had gotten loose in the storm."

I thought about it. "And they rode straight back the way they came," I said. "If they had really lost horses, they would have kept on up the road, stopping and asking, wouldn't they?"

Mrs. Frederiksen nodded. "Maybe they were cattle drovers passing through—and the tornado gave Eli big ideas. I think his friends argued him out of his scheme as they were leaving here." She tucked a wisp of her white hair back into her bun. "It's been a month. I am sure they are long gone." She reached out and lifted my hair back over my shoulders. "I think Tish would love a ride. And Flynn is bound to be restless. Just be careful and be back within a few hours."

Libby banged the kettle with a tin spoon and Mrs. Frederiksen and I both turned to look at her. She was frowning, but she looked aside as though her hand had just slipped. She didn't say anything. I tried smiling at her, but she wouldn't look at me. When I was little, I never disobeyed her. And I almost never did now. I knew she hated me asking Mrs. Frederiksen if I could go instead of asking her. But she would have said no. I was sure of that.

And I *wanted* to go riding. It was the only time I ever really felt free, like the wind in my hair blew away all the worries, at least for a while. If it had been up to my sister—and it had been most of my life—I would never do anything but work.

"I won't be gone all that long," I told Libby—or Libby's backside, anyway, she had turned toward the hearth. "You won't have to do any of my work or worry a bit. I will be very careful. I promise."

She wouldn't turn to look at me. So I just took off my apron and ran to the barn. It took two minutes to get a bridle on Tish and lead her out into the aisle, and only a few more to get a halter and a lead rope on Flynn.

I led Tish close to the corral fence, then climbed the rails until I could just lean across her back and swing my leg over. It took a few minutes of sidling and fiddling to get Flynn started after us, but as I rode up the hill, we worked out a comfortable length of slack rope between the two horses. Once we had, it was wonderful.

It was a warm morning and the sky was uncommon blue—just a beautiful day. I started slow, walking the horses, then I nudged Tish into a jog and Flynn came with us. He seemed at ease being led and Tish barely noticed him. So I decided to canter them both as far as Tish could go. At first, Flynn cantered alongside, his head high. But then, when a rabbit scuttled across the road, he tossed his mane, then surged ahead, galloping.

It was wonderful, but it was clear, in about ten strides, that Tish couldn't begin to match his speed. So I pulled the lead taut, and Flynn slowed just enough to be head-to-head with her. When I finally reined in, it was because Tish was heaving. Flynn acted like he would have run another mile, flat out. And then I heard a shout—a high-pitched girl's voice.

I pulled both horses back to a walk and turned to stare. There was a rider coming toward us, cantering—she was riding a sorrel horse. She didn't rein in until she was close, but when she did, her horse stopped instantly, sliding a little, forelegs stiff. Then the girl started talking. "I saw you from our place," she said, and pointed. I followed her gesture and saw a house in the distance.

"I hope you don't mind that I just came riding out to meet you, but I've seen you once or twice now and missed my chance because I had too many chores to do and there aren't many girls who ride out here—not really *ride*. Do you know what I mean?"

I knew exactly what she meant. Most girls rode carefully and used saddles—usually sidesaddles. Or they didn't ride at all—except in carriages and wagons.

"You ride bareback, too," I said, then felt a little silly. She could see that, for heaven's sake.

But she only smiled. "I have a saddle, but I learned bareback when I was too small to use it, so now I like it better anyway. My name is Coriander Campbell. I go by Cory."

I blinked. She even had an interesting name. She was pretty, too, her long pigtails hanging straight down her back. I introduced myself.

"Would you want to ride together sometimes?"

I nodded, feeling like someone had handed me roses. Because Mrs. Frederiksen didn't hardly call on her neighbors anymore, I hadn't met them. But I liked Cory Campbell from the minute I met her. Before I knew even one single-bingle thing about her, I liked the way she kept reaching down to pat her mare's neck as she told me about her older brother and her parents.

Joseph was nineteen now. He was hard to get along with lately, but she knew he loved her. Her mother was strict but wonderful and her father was a stern man, but kind, too. When I met him—which wouldn't be today because he and Joseph had taken the wagon to get supplies in Littleton—she wanted me to be very polite. He was a stickler for manners at first. Then Cory took a breath and I was amazed at how much I knew about her already.

"Did you see the tornado?" she asked me.

I nodded. "It came right over the soddy," I told her. "I was so scared."

"It more or less followed the road past our place," she said. "We got wind, but nothing too terrible. One cow got hurt running from it."

"We lost all but three of our hens," I told her.

"Do you have milk?"

I nodded. "More than we can use."

She smiled and leaned toward me. "Ride home with me. I think my mother would happily trade hens for fresh milk. It was our milker that got hurt and she pretty much dried up—and we have chickens coming out our ears this year."

I nodded and jutted out my chin to indicate that she should lead the way.

"Want to canter?" she asked. "Does the black lead well enough for that?"

I nodded, still amazed at how friendly she was, how easy it was for her to talk to a stranger.

"Good," she said. "I am trying to get Merry Christmas ready for the race on Harvest Day." She smiled at me. "It's at our place this year. My mother will be cooking for days before. We're already cleaning up and getting ready." She reached down and patted her horse once more.

Merry Christmas? Had the mare been a Christmas present? I exhaled, trying not to be jealous. I knew

Cory hadn't chosen her parents and her life any more than I had chosen mine. And she was just a neighbor, trying to be friendly, not some stranger trying to show off.

"There's a race?" I finally managed.

She nodded. "There's an entry fee and the winner gets to keep everyone else's. Usually twenty or thirty dollars."

I was about to ask her if she was just teasing, but she was already leaning forward and her mare leaped into a gallop. Flynn was ready to follow, but Tish took a little urging and trotted a ways before she cantered, then took even more time to extend her neck and actually gallop. So we were pretty far behind, with me hauling on the lead rope to keep Flynn back. Cory reined in on the long lane that led from the road to her house and waited for us.

It was a nice place—and the elms were tall and wide. Most of their stock was under them, enjoying the shade. The house was huge—but then almost any house would seem big after living in Mrs. Frederiksen's soddy. Cory's mother was pretty, too, and she came out onto the porch when Cory called to her. After we were introduced and had exchanged niceties, I had no idea what else to say. She asked me where I lived and I explained that my sister and I were staying with Mrs. Frederiksen. Then I waited, feeling my stomach knot up. But she didn't ask a single question about whether we were family or anything else.

"Please give Elsie my regards," she said. "She missed last year. Tell her we expect her on Harvest Day. And you and your sister, of course," she added. I nodded and smiled and still didn't know what to say, so Cory asked her about trading milk for hens.

"We have more than we can use," I added. I knew I should ask Mrs. Frederiksen before I agreed to anything, but I was truly sure it would be fine. Why would she prefer throwing out sour curds to having new hens?

"How is Mrs. Frederiksen doing?" Cory's mother asked me as she led the way to their chicken coop. "I have been thinking it was about time I went and visited."

"She is well," I said. "She works like a mule all day long. She's so nice and I just love her." I had not expected that last part to come out of my mouth, but once it had, I knew it was true. I was beginning to love Mrs. Frederiksen.

Mrs. Campbell's eyes crinkled at the corners. "Everyone who knows her thinks very well of her." She smiled. "You'll be able to tell your children you lived in a soddy," she said. "They are disappearing one by one." She pointed toward the chicken coop. "We still keep ours up, patch and mend once a year. Cory was born in it." I was puzzled for an instant, then I saw the sod house back behind it. It was even smaller that Mrs. Frederiksen's.

"We use it for a foaling barn now," Mrs. Campbell said. "It's still cooler in summer and warmer in winter than the big house will ever be."

I nodded. Mrs. Frederiksen's soddy was cozy and cool, both.

"Every hen I have set eggs this spring," Mrs. Campbell said as we got closer. Then she glanced at me. "How many do you need?"

I thought about it. "We lost eight in the tornado."

"Shall we start with a grown layer and five pullets? They'll all be laying in a month. And you and Cory can decide who will ride the milk here once a day? Or every other day?"

Cory and I both nodded at the same time and she caught my eye and winked. Had she thought about that before she had brought me here? It was perfect for me—I wanted excuses to ride. And I wanted to find out more about the race.

"I'll ride you home," Cory said, but her mother shook her head. "I need your help today. But tomorrow you can." Mrs. Campbell looked up at me. "Can you manage this, leading the gelding, too? I can put three in each of the flour sacks, then tie the tops together."

I nodded, knowing it would be awkward, but sure I would be fine if I was careful. Tish barely needed guidance to get home from here and Flynn had been calm and good, too. They both stood very still while Mrs. Campbell caught up the hens, then knotted the sacks together.

"Here you go." She lifted the bags gently and draped them over Tish's withers. Tish didn't move a muscle and the hens were quiet. So long as I didn't jostle them, they probably wouldn't make a sound all the way home. I said my good-byes and promised to bring milk the next day.

As I rode back down the lane I felt so happy I wanted to gallop all the way home. But I knew that would scare the poor chickens half to death, so I let Tish walk along at her own pace. The sun was warming up and I found myself talking to Flynn. I asked him if he would want to enter a race and he tossed his head. "Does that mean yes?" I asked him. He shook his head this time, shooing flies, but it looked like he was saying no. I laughed. "If we could win that much money, I might be able to buy you from your real owner."

And just thinking about that made me happier than I can describe. Maybe Flynn could really be mine!

About half a mile from the soddy, because I was daydreaming about the race and imagining having Flynn as my very own and barely watching the road, Tish saw a rattlesnake before I did.

It was a big one, just sleeping in the warm dust—and when it felt the hoofbeats it coiled up for a second, then just slid away into the grass. But it made Tish shy and I wasn't ready for it. The chickens set up a squawk and that startled her into turning in a circle, which tangled up the lead rope. It was taut across my leg—and I couldn't get her back around. So there was nothing for me to do but drop the rope, put the sacks over my own shoulder, then slide off.

"The snake is long gone, Tish," I scolded her, grabbing the halter rope from the ground, then backing away to lay the bags gently in the grass. Then I sorted out the rope, hanging on to the gelding while Tish snorted and pawed, pulling at the reins. "Flynn isn't scared," I chided her. "And you know better. The snake is *gone*, Tish."

I looked around, hoping for a tree or a ditch or a big enough rock—anything that would make Tish lower, or me higher, so I could get back on her.

There wasn't anything in sight. I guess I should have been upset, but I was so happy about meeting Cory and the idea that I would have a reason to ride with her, that I wasn't. Not a bit.

Tish snorted once more, then lowered her head and sniffed at the ground. Behind me, the hens were clucking, poor things. I lifted the flour sacks carefully and draped them over Tish's withers again. I took one last look round, for anything I could climb, then I faced the horses.

"Can you kneel?" I asked Tish. "No? Then perhaps Mr. Flynn? Would you kneel, please?" I made a bow and swept my right hand outward like I was holding a wide skirt as I curtsied. "No? Then I suppose we should just start walk—" And then I hushed and gripped the rope because Flynn was suddenly backing up, as though I had scared him. But he wasn't shying.

Flynn was bending one front leg, then the other. He was *kneeling*, in that awkward way that horses always do. I was so astonished that it took me a long, dumbstruck moment to walk over to him, swing a leg over his back, straddling his withers, Tish's reins in my hand.

The moment I was in place, he lurched to the right, then the left as he stood up. I barely stayed on, grabbing his mane to steady myself. Tish was watching, interested, no longer thinking about the snake. I had a moment of fear that I couldn't control Flynn with just the halter. I knew if I walked the horses a few steps, got them close together, that I could stop again, then lean out and slide onto Tish's back. But Flynn was so still, so calm, that I touched his sides with my bare heels, and he started walking.

Tish clopped along beside him, her head high for a moment, then she calmed once we had passed the place where the snake had been. The chickens stayed quiet, too, and I was grateful.

And all the way home I tried to imagine a cowboy who would have known how to teach a horse to kneel—or who had a reason to. Could it have been a rancher or a soldier or some fancy horse breeder from back east? Why? I couldn't imagine how it was done, either. With a dog, you just said *sit* or *shake* over and over, pushing its bottom down or lifting its paw until it understood what you wanted. How would anyone teach a horse to kneel? And who would want to?

Once we were closer to the soddy, I drew the horses together, flank to flank, and slid from Flynn's back onto Tish's. Then I guided them both up the path.

"Where did you come from?" I asked Flynn once I had gotten him and Tish back in the pasture.

He tossed his head and I rubbed his forelock and hoped I would never know. Finding out would mean meeting the person who owned him.

Mrs. Frederiksen was delighted with the trade. She made a fuss over the hens—they were taller and weightier than the ones she'd had and the pullets weren't even all the way grown yet. "Once Mrs. Campbell feels paid in full for these," she said, "see if you can trade for a rooster. Then we can raise our own again next year."

I nodded and glanced at Libby. Next year. Next year I still wanted to be right here. Lib had been watching me carefully as I described the Campbell place and told her what I had learned about the family. Her face was stiff and expressionless, which could mean anything at all. Sometimes she just thought I was frivolous and had little interest in what I was saying. Other times, a stiff face meant she was upset and trying to hide it.

I know it sounds mean, but, for once, I honestly didn't much care what Lib was thinking. I'd had a wonderful day and I didn't want to ruin it worrying about what my sister thought about it.

Later, when Mrs. Frederiksen and I were out in the garden taking turns turning the dirt, I asked her if she knew about the horse race. She nodded and wiped her hands on her apron. "I do. It's usually one of the older boys who wins. We had one girl, some years back. Once in a while a grown man wins the purse. But usually they're too heavy—it's a two-mile race."

"Purse? Do you mean the prize?" I asked.

"Usually around twenty dollars," she said. "Sometimes closer to thirty."

I caught my breath. So it was true, and Cory hadn't been exaggerating. If I could win the race before Flynn's owner showed up, maybe I could buy him. Mrs. Frederiksen smiled at me before she went back to spading and I was pretty sure she had guessed my thoughts.

Lying on my pallet that night next to Libby's, I realized I hadn't told her or Mrs. Frederiksen about Flynn kneeling. I thought about it. Why not? And why had I switched horses coming home? The truth was that I wanted to keep Flynn's trick a secret—for some reason I couldn't name. And that is exactly what I did.

CHAPTER SEVEN

❧ ❧ ❧

The next morning, I flew through my chores. I used Mrs. Campbell's flour sacks to rig up a simple carrier for the tight-lidded honey tins Mrs. Frederiksen had filled with milk. Once we had them ready, Mrs. Frederiksen walked out onto the porch with me and bowed and stretched, saying her good morning to her husband and the sun.

"Looking forward to your ride?" she asked me when she was finished.

I nodded. "Flynn was so good yesterday," I told her, "I am going to ride him today."

She turned to look at me. "You sure?"

I nodded. "He was perfect. We even saw a snake and he barely shied. It was Tish that was hard to handle for a minute or two."

Mrs. Frederiksen pushed my hair back and kissed the top of my head. "You just be careful."

"I want to enter the race," I told her quietly so Libby wouldn't be able to hear from inside the kitchen.

Mrs. Frederiksen nodded. "I thought as much. And I don't see why not if you are careful. There are always a few your age in it. They run it on the road so there's no danger of prairie-dog holes or uneven ground, and they block it off so there's no danger of a carriage or riders getting in the way."

I glanced at the soddy door. Mrs. Frederiksen sighed. "What if Libby doesn't want you to?"

I shrugged, started to answer, then stopped. I didn't know what I would do. I didn't want to disobey Lib. It felt wrong—I knew she loved me and only wanted me safe. But I had to race Flynn. How else could I ever earn enough money to buy him?

"Also, there's a two-dollar entry fee," Mrs. Frederiksen said.

I blinked. We had a little money, but not that much. Besides, Libby kept it and I knew she would never approve of me spending a single penny of it to ride in a horse race.

"Work things out with your sister, if you can. Get her permission. But I ought to pay you something for making the trade and riding the milk back and forth," Mrs. Frederiksen said. "We can think of ways for you to earn the rest."

"You don't have to pay me for anything," I began, and I meant it. A lot of people had taken us in, all my life, but no one else had ever made me feel like I really belonged there, like it might really be my home. I felt my eyes sting. "I can't let you—" But she waved one hand to hush me before I could finish.

"You do more than your share here, Miss Margret. I haven't touched a milk bucket or a pitchfork since you arrived. You'll have your entry fee."

I looked into her eyes. I didn't want pity money, but I desperately wanted to enter the race. "I will earn it," I said.

"I know you will." She put her hand out and we shook, like two men would, making a deal.

Flynn was glad to see me, nickering when I came into the barn, then putting his head over the stall gate so I could rub his forehead and his ears. He stood like a stone while I bridled him and arranged the flour-sack carrier. The milk sloshed in the tins and swung back and forth a little, but it didn't seem to bother him. He sidled close to the stall rails when I nudged him that way so I could climb up high enough to get on his back.

"How long will you be gone?" Libby called into the barn. I turned, startled.

"A few hours at most," I answered. She was standing just outside the wide double doors. Her voice sounded sharp. Tense.

"Be careful," she said.

"I promise I will," I said. "Flynn is really gentle and he doesn't seem to shy at anything. And I —"

"Mrs. Frederiksen said something about a horse race," Libby interrupted. "I don't want you riding in it." Even though I couldn't see her face against the glare of the morning sun, I knew her lips were tight and her brows were drawn.

I took a quick breath and I felt my temper rising, then I forced myself to smile again. "It sounded like it would be fun," I said aloud.

She didn't answer. Without another word, she walked away. I just sat still on Flynn and counted to a hundred, rubbing his neck and fiddling with his mane. I had almost three weeks. Once she had seen me galloping on Flynn nearly every day, once she got used to nothing bad coming of it, maybe she would relent. I bit my lip. Or maybe she would use the race as an excuse to leave. I shivered, even though I wasn't chilly. I wanted Cory to be my friend. I had never really had a friend. We moved around too much. And we had fibbed too much, I thought suddenly. When we were keeping things to ourselves, not trusting anyone, it had been impossible to have any real friends.

I rode up the path and called out a good-bye as I passed the soddy. Mrs. Frederiksen came out onto the porch. "Don't forget to give Mrs. Campbell my best wishes."

I nodded. I could hear Libby banging pots. She didn't come out. I sat up straighter as I rode down the path to the road. Somehow, I had to make Libby see what a good place for us this really was, how much like a real grandmother Mrs. Frederiksen could be to us—if Libby would just give her a chance.

Riding Flynn down the road, I didn't dare let him trot, much less gallop. The milk tins would swing and bounce, and maybe stampede him. But it was still wonderful to be riding him. The morning was bright and fresh and the sunlight was warm on my back. Birds were singing and a light wind came up, making the grass whistle and sigh.

It took a long time to get to the Campbells' place—or maybe it just seemed long because I was excited and I had to ride so slowly. Cory was out in front when I got there, walking back from their barn. I waved to let her know I saw her, but I didn't nudge Flynn into a jog. I had come the whole way walking and I wasn't about to chance him shying now.

Cory took the tins and set them down. "My mother likes you," she said as I slid off Flynn's back.

It pleased me no end that she would say that first, before anything else. "I'm glad," I said. I felt silly, but the truth was, I very much wanted the whole Campbell family to like me. I wanted to be Cory's friend.

When we carried the milk into the kitchen, Mrs. Campbell looked up and smiled at me—a big, warm, friendly smile. I thought about Libby—grumpy and angry and banging pots and pans around. I knew what she would say if she were here. She would tell me that the Campbells weren't as nice or as friendly as they seemed, and that before long, they would be unkind to us—that they weren't family. I pushed the thought away. I loved my sister, but I wasn't like her. The scratchy squeaking of a young rooster just learning to crow made me glance out the door.

"Do you think you might have a rooster to spare after we settle our first bargain?" I asked Mrs. Campbell.

She laughed. "Right now I wouldn't mind trading the whole batch to anyone who wanted them. Last full moon, they were crowing all night long. We barely slept."

I nodded. Roosters were *loud*. The soddy walls were so thick that we had barely heard Mrs. Frederiksen's rooster, but the Gleasons had carried two hens and a rooster in a wood crate nailed to the side of their wagon. None of us ever slept until dawn. Like all roosters, as soon as the stars dimmed, he was crowing.

"Come with me," Mrs. Campbell said. "You can pick one out now."

I tied Flynn to their hitching rail and followed her, Cory walking beside me. When we got to her henhouse, I stopped, staring at the roosters in a side pen. There were twenty or more and I knew most of them would end up in a stew pot. No one had reason to keep that many roosters. There were whites, and reds and blacks, and two with black-and-white feathers that looked almost like checked gingham. Mrs. Campbell looked back and forth between me and the pen. "You like the Barred Rocks? My father had them back in Connecticut.

I brought two hens and a rooster with me when we came out here and I get a few with that coloring every year. I want to keep all the pullets, but if you want a rooster, you can have it."

"They are sure pretty," I said.

She nodded. "And they're strong and sturdy and the hens lay well and set well."

I watched her catch one. He was beautiful. I knew Mrs. Frederiksen would love him.

"Mother?"

I turned to see Cory's brother striding toward us. He waited until he was close, then introduced himself politely to me and asked Cory if she was going to ride me home. He chided her to be careful.

"I always am, Joseph."

He made a face at her and winked at me. Then he turned back to his mother. "Father asks if you managed to patch his work trousers while we were gone."

"I did," she said, and told him where to look. I watched him walk away. Cory was pretty and Joseph was handsome. An older brother might be even better than an older sister as far as a friend for Libby was concerned. I wondered if Joseph would be dancing on Harvest Day—and if he already had a sweetheart.

Then, having thought that, I wondered if Mrs. Frederiksen had some cloth we could make into a nice dress for Libby. She was very pretty when she was smiling. I admit it was a selfish thought—I wanted her to have a reason to stay here because I wanted to stay. But it was the best kind of selfish thought. Because I knew if she had a boy sweet on her, she would be much happier. At least that's what I told myself.

Joseph walked with us back to the house. I set the flour sack on the porch, then scrambled onto the hitching rail to mount. When I looked up, Cory was on Merry's back, talking to her brother. He handed me the flour sacks, then went in. Cory and I rode down their lane, side by side. We let the horses amble along. I kept asking her questions so that she wouldn't ask me any. I didn't mean to. It was a habit and it took me a long while to realize what I was doing.

A mile up the road, the rooster decided to pitch a fit. He fought the flour sack, trying to flap his wings, clawing at the cloth. I held the sack away from Flynn's shoulder and kept a tight rein, just in case, but he never shied. And after a minute or two, the rooster settled. I promised him he would like his new home and looked up to see Cory staring at Flynn.

"He's sure good," she said. "And a beauty, too. Where did you get him? Or is he Mrs. Frederiksen's?"

I looked off at the horizon for an instant, wondering what I should tell her. Then I bit my lip and made a big decision. All my life Libby had taught me to lie about certain things—and I was in the habit of it. But I didn't want to lie to Cory. I wanted to be her friend. So I explained about the tornado, about finding Flynn. I didn't tell her about him kneeling, but mostly because she interrupted with questions about his wound and what we had done to help it heal. When I was finished, she told me what her father did when a horse got cut. Then she went on, talking about what a good animal doctor he was. Then she was quiet for a minute or two.

"It must be awful thinking that someone could just ride up any day and claim Flynn." She broke the silence in a quiet voice. Then she met my eyes. "I won't say anything to my parents—or Joseph—unless you tell me to."

I thanked her. "That's why I want to win the race, Cory. So if his real owner shows up, I can buy Flynn with the prize money." I paused and combed Flynn's mane with my fingers, feeling my eyes sting. "I really love him," I said, hoping she wouldn't laugh at me.

She didn't.

"I love Merry," she said. "She listens to me complain about my brother when he gets bossy. Whenever I am upset about anything, I can always go out to the barn and find a friend."

I nodded and we looked at each other for a long moment.

Then she smiled. "We could start galloping together every day, getting our horses ready for the race."

I nodded slowly. "I can bring the milk, then you can ride me home and we'll give them a good run. I won't be able to do more than that. I have too many chores."

"I do, too," she said. "But whatever we can manage will be good for them both. Joseph won't ride with me much anymore. He's too grown up, I guess. Besides, he's almost always with Papa now." She made a face.

"Is he going to be in the race?" I asked her.

She shook her head. "He won last year. You have to sit out a year if you win."

"That's fair to the rest," I said.

Cory nodded. "It is. But Joseph doesn't like it." She grinned. "Guess I wouldn't, either."

I looked up the road and saw that we were nearly there. I tried to think of some way to have Cory go home without meeting Libby or finding out about our lives—all the wandering we had done—then I caught myself again. I had told her the truth about Flynn. If I let her find out everything else, I could just be honest and never worry about lying to her again.

"There you are!" Mrs. Frederiksen called out as we came up the rise. She stood on the porch waiting for us to get down and tie the horses to the hitching rail. Cory said a polite hello and Mrs. Frederiksen said nice things about her blue eyes and her pretty smile and how much she had grown since Mrs. Frederiksen had seen her last.

Libby didn't come out. I thought about going inside to get her, but then Mrs. Frederiksen got Cory talking about her family and her place, and when I told her I had brought a rooster like none she had never seen before, we all walked around to the side of the soddy. I went inside the coop and laid the sack down gently and untied the end. The rooster came blustering out and strutted around, sizing up the place. The hens crowded around him, clucking.

"You're right. I have never seen anything like him," Mrs. Frederiksen said. "He's a beauty."

She turned to Cory. "Please thank your mother for me."

And it was then that I glanced up and saw Libby standing at the corner of the soddy, staring at us. I jumped up and called her name and went to bring her around to the coop. I was kind of pulling at her, making her come whether she wanted to or not. She didn't turn it into a fight—maybe she didn't want to be embarrassed in front of Cory. Whatever her reason, she let me nudge her along, and once she was standing beside the chicken coop, I let go of her arm. Then I held my breath.

Cory was so friendly and so nice that Libby had to smile twice. Mrs. Frederiksen was glancing between us as Cory talked. When her eyes met mine, she winked, so quick I wasn't sure I had seen it. Then Cory sighed. "I guess I should start home. Margret said she has chores every day and so do I. But we want to ride whenever we can." She looked up at Mrs. Frederiksen.

I nodded and refused to so much as glance at Libby. "Can I ride her a little ways back?" I asked.

Mrs. Frederiksen pretended to scowl. "And she then will ride you home, then you can ride her home, and you two will never get off those horses again?" That made us all laugh.

"Go," Mrs. Frederiksen said to me. "Get your gallop in for the day. But not too far and hurry back. Libby is making double-batch bread today and we all have to take turns kneading." She looked at Libby. "How long before you want help?"

Libby looked startled by the question, but I could tell she was happy to be the one to decide how long I could be gone.

"The dough will have risen before an hour is up."

Cory and I ran back around the house to the hitching rail. I started to lead Flynn to the porch, but Cory laced her fingers together and showed me how to step into them like a stirrup. Just as I stepped up, she boosted me up high enough to swing my leg over Flynn's back. I was up so fast it made me laugh. Then she did something that looked like magic to me. She reached up and got a handful of Merry's mane with her left hand, then backed up a half step and swung up onto her back.

She just . . . swung up.

"You have to teach me how to do that," I said. I *meant* to say it anyway, I actually whispered it. That's how amazed I was.

"Joseph taught me. He'll show you," Cory promised.

We jogged down Mrs. Frederiksen's little hill, then, once we were a little ways from the soddy, Cory let Merry have her head and she rose into a canter. Flynn switched his tail and broke into a canter, too, without any signal from me. The morning was still cool and there was a little breeze that was making them both frisky. Flynn flattened out and lengthened his stride into a gallop without me doing anything but sitting there. I laughed and let him go. Merry stretched her neck out, too, and they pounded along, racing each other for the fun of it.

After about a mile, I reined in and Cory did, too, and we pulled our horses back to a walk. Cory's cheeks were flushed and she was smiling. "If there is any feeling finer than that," she said quietly, "I can't imagine it."

I sighed. "I better get back."

Laughing, Cory turned Merry around and I followed her, both of us pretending that Mrs. Frederiksen's joke about riding forever was going to come true. Then she turned to me. "Are you and Libby Mrs. Frederiksen's granddaughters?"

She was smiling, but it caught me off guard and I instantly felt the familiar weight in my stomach. "Our parents died when I was really little," I said quietly. "I don't remember them. Libby has always looked out for us both. We're just staying with Mrs. Frederiksen for a while."

Cory blinked twice. Then she exhaled. "My younger brother died two years back of a terrible fever. I miss him every single day—I cry in the barn where no one has to hear me. It's still so hard for my parents." She slid her hand down to pat Merry's neck.

We rode in silence another minute or two. Then she reined in and smiled at me. "It's very nice to have a new friend," she said.

I nodded. "I hope we can stay with Mrs. Frederiksen a long time."

"I do, too," she said. Then we rode in silence for a few more minutes before we parted ways.

I felt as good as I had ever felt. In my whole life, I mean. I hadn't lied, and Cory hadn't pitied me, because she understood. Maybe that was why we didn't bother to say much more to each other that day. We had already told each other the deepest thing we could.

CHAPTER EIGHT

❦ ❦ ❦

Cory and I rode together every time I delivered milk. And every time I saw her father, I was careful to be very polite. Joseph was always friendly and her mother was wonderful. I loved going there. But Cory and I didn't get to gallop together as much as we wanted because I was either carrying milk or empty honey tins. Then Cory and I worked out a pattern. Wednesdays, Flynn and I carried milk to her house, as early as we could get there. Fridays and Mondays, she came to get it, bringing back the empty tins. On my day, she would ride me home—at a gallop. On hers, we rode for an hour or more, going east on the road, galloping all we could. Then, when she had to start back, we would fill the milk tins for her to carry back at a walk. Usually, I rode with her a ways, then galloped most of the way home, pretending I was racing, imagining horses all around us. Flynn was getting stronger and stronger. And he loved to run.

On the days between, I worked hard, starting chores before dawn, taking time out to gallop Flynn on the road in the evenings. One day, when we were out of sight of the soddy, I asked him to kneel again, just to see if he would. He did. I saw a nick on one of his knees the next day and I felt terrible. I apologized to him over and over—and I promised him I would learn to get on him myself. I tried swinging up but I couldn't figure it out. I ended up falling flat on my back a few times and finally gave up. I really wanted to learn before Harvest Day. I didn't want to have to lead Flynn to a fence to get on him if all the other riders knew how to swing up.

One day, riding with milk-filled honey tins to Cory's house, I saw her come running out, breathless and smiling. Her father was right behind her, on his way to the barn.

"Nice to see you, Miss Margret," he said. I said hello and bade him a good day and he smiled, looking at Flynn. "That's a good-looking animal," he said quietly. Then he looked at me. "You are both going to ride in the race?"

I nodded. "Yes, sir."

He smiled. "You two don't let it get in the way of your friendship."

"We won't," Cory said with so much certainty that I could only smile at her as her father walked away. We took the milk in, then started back out. On the porch, Cory stopped. "Wait. I should go tell my mother we're about to leave." She ran back inside, banging the door shut behind her.

"My sister doesn't mean to be rude." Joseph's voice startled me and I turned to see him walking toward me, coming from one of the outbuildings. His nose was pink from the crisp morning air. "She just gets excited about things and forgets that she shouldn't leave a guest standing on the porch."

"She just ran in to ask if she could ride back with me. We're practicing . . . " I trailed off, remembering that he couldn't race this year.

He nodded. "I know. She has told me you are both racing. Three or four times."

I blinked, not knowing if he was teasing or not. "We are both pretty excited."

"That's a good horse, " Joseph said, echoing what his father had said.

"Will you teach me to swing up?" I asked, and I felt my cheeks get hot. "If you don't mind, I mean."

He smiled. "It isn't that hard."

Just then, Cory came out of the house. "I'll get Merry!" she said. I watched her run toward the barn, her dress flared out behind her, her petticoats showing.

"Quite the proper young lady, our Cory," Joseph said, shaking his head, then he looked at me again. "She says you have an older sister?"

I nodded.

"Cory told me she is pretty and seems very nice," he said.

I nodded again.

"Please tell her we never have enough girls at the Harvest Day dance. The boys end up dancing with their sisters half the night."

"I will tell her," I promised.

Joseph arched his brows at me. "Ready?"

I nodded.

He walked over to Flynn and patted him for a moment, then he stepped back and swung up, just like Cory had, except he was even more graceful about it.

I tried and couldn't get my right foot even halfway up Flynn's side.

"Like this," Joseph said.

He showed me again, much slower. His left hand grasping Flynn's mane, he stepped back and pivoted on his left foot, kicking a high arc with his right, swinging in a half circle around the hand clutching Flynn's mane. "It's getting the angle right more than anything," he said.

I tried again and he stood close enough to catch me when I slid off. Then he stepped back and patted Flynn. "This time take that first step like you are starting a footrace."

I tried again. Then again. And again. Cory came back from the barn, leading Merry, but she just reined in and didn't say a word.

I looked at Joseph. He wasn't laughing at me. He wasn't even smiling. "You're close," he said. "Catch your breath, walk away for a minute, then walk back like you are about to leave and just swing up the way you would slide off. Don't think about it much, just do it."

I nodded and did exactly what he said. When I walked back to Flynn, I untied the reins and put them over his neck. Then I swung up. Really. I did! I swung up and I was on his back!

Joseph whooped and Cory clapped her hands. They were both grinning at me. I felt wonderful, sitting on top of Flynn, smiling back at them.

"Now," Joseph said, "*now* you can go riding." He looked at Cory. "Shall we tell her that it took you almost a week to get it?"

Cory looked up at the sky, pretending to think about what he had said. Then she looked at me and smiled. "No. Margret and I are honest with each other." She sighed. "It was two weeks."

I laughed aloud. And I was still smiling when Cory and I trotted back down their lane. "Papa said it's best to jog them for a while before we gallop," she told me.

"Joseph showed me something else," she said as we started up the road. "Watch how I sit once we get going."

I nodded and held Flynn to a jog until Cory glanced at me. "That should be enough. Papa said five or ten minutes." She reined in. "And Joseph said we should practice starting." Cory slid off Merry's back and handed me her reins while she scraped a line in the dirt from one side of the road to the other.

We took turns counting off the start. Flynn had it figured out on the fourth try. It was as though he understood the words *ready, set, go!* All I had to do was be ready for his lunge forward.

On our fourth practice start, we just kept going, giving the horses their heads and pounding down a long straight stretch of the road. I glanced at Cory and I saw what she had been talking about. She was sitting just behind Merry's withers. And she was leaning forward over the mare's neck.

I slid up and shifted my weight forward. It felt odd at first, but Flynn seemed to run freer, with less effort. It was amazing. I hadn't moved more than a few inches, really, but it felt right, like Flynn and I were galloping together.

Merry and Flynn ran head-to-head almost the whole way back to the soddy. Neither Cory nor I was really trying to race, and our horses seemed content to have a tie, too. Once they were at a hard gallop, they more or less matched each other's stride. They might as well have been harnessed and hitched together—that's how close they kept.

Both horses were blowing out long breaths and their shoulders were wet with sweat when we finally reined in. Cory's cheeks were pink and I wondered if I looked as happy as she did. We said our good-byes while the horses caught their wind. "Tell your mother I'll bring more milk Wednesday," I told Cory, and she started off home.

I walked Flynn the rest of the way, letting him cool off, his breathing slow. I stopped at the soddy and made Lib and Mrs. Frederiksen come out and watch me swing up. Mrs. Frederiksen smiled and looked amazed. Lib wasn't quite as enthusiastic, but she smiled and I was grateful. They both shook their heads in amazement and made me feel wonderful.

I turned Flynn out into the pasture and led Tish and Bennie out to graze, then Bessie, too. I hadn't carried water up before I left, so I went to get the bucket. When I came in, Libby nodded at me without saying a word, then pointed at the tin tub steaming on the hearth. I knew what that meant. Mrs. Frederiksen had declared a Bath Day. I traipsed back and forth to the well six times, setting the full buckets against the wall.

Libby went first, sitting in the bathtub, her knees bent so sharp her chin nearly rested on them. We scrubbed each other's back and combed out each other's hair and put on clean clothes. When we were finished, we went outside and Mrs. Frederiksen went in. "You two look beautiful," she said before she closed the door.

That reminded me. "Cory's older brother asked me to tell you there are never enough girls at the Harvest Day dance."

Libby had been braiding her damp hair. She looked up. "What?"

"I guess Cory told him you were pretty and nice."

Libby made a face. "I'm neither one."

"You are always pretty," I told her, "and you are nice most of the time. I want you to go."

She shook her head. "I am not going to. I can't dance and I don't want to see the race." She looked at me. "What if you get hurt? It's bad enough, all the riding you are doing now. I wish you would just stop."

I was quiet for a long time, dragging the comb through my hair. I had no idea what to say. I thought she would get used to me riding Flynn, but I was still afraid she would forbid me to race him. But she hadn't. Maybe she knew that I wouldn't obey her this time. But even if she didn't forbid me to go, I was so disappointed that she wouldn't come that I was afraid I might start crying. I turned to face her.

"Lib, I want you to go. I want us both to just have fun for once. And I want you to see me and Flynn win. Or lose. I just want you to *be* there." When she didn't answer, I took a long breath, trying to think of a way to convince her. But I couldn't.

CHAPTER NINE

❦ ❦ ❦

A week before Harvest Day, after I had gotten back from galloping Flynn, Lib and I were shelling beans on the front porch when she looked up. "Can you hear that?"

And as soon as she said it, I heard faint hoofbeats and distant voices. The voices were high, excited. Children. We set down our baskets and walked around the soddy so we could look. As we passed the chicken coop, the new hens clucked a little and the rooster strutted to assure them that he would protect them if we meant harm. He was very vain and I had been right about Mrs. Frederiksen making a pet out of him. He took bits of bread from the palm of her hand.

"A carriage," Lib said, and I nodded.

We saw farm wagons a few times a week, but there had never been a fancy carriage out here. The horse was trotting smartly, its head high.

"A nice carriage with a man, his wife, and what looks like two children in it."

I nodded and this time I understood her. We hurried back to the porch and Lib went inside to tell Mrs. Fredericksen. She came out, smiling. "It's my birthday. I hoped they might come." She glanced from me to Lib, then back. "I am going to clean up a little. If they get here before I am finished, explain yourselves any way you care to, ladies, and tell them I will be out in a few minutes." Then she went back in.

Libby and I sat nervously, hoping Mrs. Frederiksen would hurry, but, of course, she didn't. We heard the carriage slow, the wheels creaking as it made the turn on to the uphill path that led from the road to the house.

The woman tilted her head when she saw Libby and me. Their children stared, too. The boy was four or five, the girl maybe seven or eight. I looked at the woman's fine-boned hands and her high cheekbones and knew this was Mrs. Frederiksen's daughter. There were mare's-tail reeds and mustard flowers in a loose bundle on the seat. They had stopped to pick wildflowers. There was a wicker basket, too. A picnic? My mouth watered and I blushed. I hadn't eaten since early morning.

"Hello!" the man called out as he reined the team in.

I nodded and so did Libby, but neither of us said anything. Libby's face was tight, stiff. The man climbed down, then helped his wife to the ground. The little boy jumped down and pushed past him and ran straight on down the hill into the little grove of trees. I heard him laugh aloud, then saw a few birds fly out of the branches, startled. The boy ran back, circling the soddy. I heard the chickens clucking and knew he was looking at the new rooster.

The girl let her father lift her down, then smoothed her skirt with her hands. It was pretty, a deep blue cloth with flower shapes embroidered along the hem. She had a hat on, like her mother, like they were on their way to church. I took a breath and was about to introduce myself and Libby when I felt a tug on my sleeve. The boy had gone all the way around the house and crept onto the porch.

"Where's Grandmother?" he asked from behind me.

"She is inside," I told him. "She will be out in a few minutes."

"Who are you?" he demanded.

His mother came closer. "Don't be rude, Caleb. I am sure they are friends of your grandmother's."

"She has been very kind to us and—" I began.

"And we have been doing all the chores," Libby interrupted.

"She has let us stay here," I finished.

The woman looked back and forth between us. "I am Colleen McKenzie, Mrs. Frederiksen's daughter."

"She just told us this is her birthday," I added, then felt silly. Of course Mrs. McKenzie knew it was her mother's birthday.

But she only smiled. "You are both living here with my mother now?"

I nodded.

"I am very glad to know that," Mrs. McKenzie said.

I blinked. I wasn't sure what I had been expecting, but her smile and the warmth in her voice startled me a little. I don't know why. She was just like her mother. Kind.

"We have been trying to talk my mother into coming to live in Denver City with us," she said. "Has she told you that?"

I nodded. "She doesn't want to leave—" and then I stopped and glanced back at the soddy door. I had been about to say something out loud that was not my business to say. My mouth was half open. I closed it.

Mrs. McKenzie nodded and leaned close to whisper. "My father. I know." She sighed. "I understand, but I worry about her." She straightened up. "I will worry less knowing you two are here."

"Thank you," I said, and hoped she knew what I meant—that I was glad she trusted us. I glanced at Libby, wondering what she was thinking. I already knew the truth. Mrs. McKenzie wasn't looking for a way to take advantage of us—and she never would. I knew Libby would say we just didn't know her yet, and of course that was true. But I could *tell*. Why couldn't Libby?

Before anyone could say anything more, the soddy door opened and Mrs. Frederiksen came out, her face washed and her hair redone, her tortoiseshell combs holding it close to the nape of her neck as always.

"Graaammaw!" Caleb shouted.

"Caaaaaaaleb!" Mrs. Frederiksen yelled back at him.

He ran to her and nearly knocked her over with his hug. The girl was behind him, waiting her turn, her arms wide. "And my lovely Ruth," Mrs. Frederiksen said. She kissed them both on top of their heads, and hugged them for a long time, her eyes closed. Then she introduced Libby and me and said we were guests. "And I'm hoping that they will just stay on," she added. "I have so enjoyed their company and appreciated their help."

I was looking at Libby when Mrs. Frederiksen said it, and there was a flicker of something in Lib's eyes—she hadn't expected Mrs. Frederiksen to say anything that nice. But then we all nodded at one another, smiling like strangers do when no one knows what to say next.

Then Mrs. Frederiksen went into the soddy, pulling her grandchildren with her, telling them she had fresh milk or ice-cold water, whichever they wanted.

"I'm not sure we will be here much longer," Libby said quietly, turning to face Mrs. McKenzie. I caught my breath.

"Oh, I hope you will," Mrs. McKenzie said. "I can't tell you how much better I would feel knowing my mother isn't alone. And it isn't that far from the Littleton school. A group of children all ride together, I think. They used to, anyway. And my mother taught school years ago. If the snow piles up, you can have your lessons here."

Libby arched her eyebrows and I wondered if Cory was just assuming we would start school in the fall, too. We were both so excited about the race, we hadn't talked about much else. *School.* I would be way behind, I was sure. And Lib was almost too old.

Mrs. McKenzie was still smiling, but I saw her glance at Libby. My sister's face had stiffened. "I am not at all sure we will be staying," she said again.

Mrs. McKenzie sighed. "Is there anything I could do to ensure it? I would be happy to pay you something to stay on."

"Your mother," I said quietly, "has been very kind to us. We are happy to earn our keep and call the bargain even."

"What nice girls you are," Mrs. McKenzie said to me, but her smile included Libby and I was glad. "Will you help me set up the picnic dinner? My mother is useless for any kind of chore when Caleb and Ruth are nearby."

I nodded and we followed her to the carriage. Within a half hour we had cleared the sideboard of its everyday burden and had laid out a meal of fried chicken, beefsteak, creamed corn, potatoes, and fresh corn bread, honey, and butter. We filled plates, then had to sit where we could.

Mrs. Frederiksen took her grandchildren into her little bedroom, where she had covered her laced coverlet with a clean—but old—blanket. The McKenzies and Lib and I moved the little table to the porch, where we could put the chairs on all four sides. Libby wasn't saying much, and I was nervous, too.

Mrs. McKenzie ate a few bites, then looked across the table at Libby. "My mother said she hasn't cooked but once or twice since you came."

Libby nodded, but didn't answer.

"She says it's because what you make shames anything she makes," Mrs. McKenzie said, and there was a warm laugh beneath the words.

Libby nodded again, a puzzled look on her face.

"Well," Mrs. McKenzie said, "I suppose you can guess who taught me to cook. So I apologize if it isn't up to the standards of this establishment."

We all laughed. Her husband glanced at her, a look so full of love that it made me skip a breath, then take the next one, deep. I glanced at Lib. She had seen it, too, I could tell. Lib and Mrs. McKenzie ended up exchanging fried-chicken receipts and I learned more in that hour-long meal than I had ever known about cooking. The secrets to fried chicken were turning it only once in the pan and never piercing the meat with fork or knife nor salting it while it cooked. Any of these would dry it out. And the temperature of the frying grease was important, too. It could be tested by how fast a potato slice the thickness of rose petal browned.

"And I suppose your gravy is as good as everything else you make?" Mrs. McKenzie asked.

"Even better," I said, just to make Lib smile. I glanced at her. She looked embarrassed and happy, all at once.

"Well then," Mrs. McKenzie said. "Next time we do this, you'll have to promise to cook."

I remembered Mrs. Frederiksen saying Libby and I should plan a picnic. This was even better, in a way. Libby had always gotten compliments on her cooking before. But in the other places we had stayed, we had usually eaten in the kitchen while the family ate in the dining room, if there was one—or at a separate table. This was like being part of the family.

"Piecrust?" Mrs. McKenzie said wistfully, and her husband made a face that set us all laughing. Then Lib told her piecrust secrets. Hard, cold butter was the crux of it and speed with the pastry cutter. I tried to pay attention, but I was having more fun watching my sister smile and laugh.

After the food was eaten and the remainder put into keeping plates and set aside, we all sat on the porch, looking out at the sky and the grove of ash trees.

"You missed the circus, Grandmother," Caleb said into the comfortable silence that had fallen among us.

Mrs. McKenzie laughed gently. "It wasn't really a circus, Caleb. But the horses were well trained, no doubt about that. They knew lots of tricks."

I turned to look at her.

"Miss Margret is quite the horsewoman," Mrs. Frederiksen said. "You should see her swing up, bareback, just like an Indian."

I refused to look at her. I knew she wanted me to tell them about Flynn so they could ask around in Denver and I knew it was the right thing to do, but I could not make myself do it.

"Were they missing any horses?" Libby asked, and I jerked around to stare at her.

"I haven't heard anything about it," Mr. McKenzie said. "Why?"

I exhaled, glad I had never told Lib about Flynn kneeling. She would have told them all that, too, I was sure. I could feel my heart thudding. Maybe Flynn was a trick show horse. Maybe kneeling was part of the act. I was afraid to ask. I glanced at Lib. She looked smug. For an instant, I hated my sister.

"We found a gelding after the tornado," Mrs. Frederiksen was saying. "Margret has become very fond of it."

"I didn't see a thing in the newspaper, no notices nailed up. So I doubt it," Mr. McKenzie said.

Just then Caleb decided to try a somersault on the patchy grass below the porch. He managed it, more or less. I was grateful for the distraction. And when he stood up, his mother scolded him gently about dirtying his clothes. I knew what a labor laundry day was for women who had little children. Or maybe she had a laundress. If so, she was considerate of the woman's efforts. I was so relieved when they all began talking about statehood, the arguments for and against becoming part of the United States. There was talk about redrawing the counties to be smaller and Mr. McKenzie thought it was foolish.

I glanced at my sister. She was uneasy again, now that the conversation wasn't about cooking. I was so angry with her that I honestly didn't care. She knew what Flynn meant to me, and how winning the race might mean that I could keep him.

I stood up and offered to take the children for a walk. They danced and clapped and off we went.

Neither one had any interest in the barn animals, so I showed them a nest I had noticed in one of the ash trees, then we walked a little ways up the road, skipping rocks on the flat dust. All of us stopped, startled and smiling, when a rabbit hopped across in front of us. We walked a ways farther and saw hawks overhead and a king snake, fresh off a molt, gleaming cream, red, and black rings on its body. Caleb tried to catch it, but it disappeared into a thicket. Then we started back. Halfway there, Caleb sprinted ahead, yelling to us that it was a race. Ruth caught up and passed him. I went as slow as I could, letting both of them beat me.

When we got back to the soddy, Mrs. McKenzie thanked me for giving them a chance to talk without the children interrupting. I nodded. I could hear Libby, banging around in the kitchen, cleaning up.

"We stopped at Bell's House, in Littleton," Mrs. McKenzie was telling her mother. "But it has changed hands. They're calling it the Harwood Inn now. It's nice enough. So we'll stay there tonight. And we'll be back out for Harvest Day unless it rains and we can't get across the river. It's at Campbells' place this year?"

"Yes. And I hoped you would come," Mrs. Frederiksen said. "The girls and I will be going. Miss Margret plans to ride in the race. She wants to win to have a good offer for the owner whenever he shows up. Flynn dotes on her, too. That gelding whinnies every time he sees her coming."

I saw Mrs. McKenzie and her mother exchange a long look. "Flynn? Handsome, is he?"

Mrs. Frederiksen nodded, smiling. "And good-hearted."

I smiled and shuffled my feet, wishing they would talk about anything else. I didn't want Mr. McKenzie to mention Flynn to anyone in Littleton before they went back to Denver City in the morning . . . the race was so *close* now.

When they started their good-byes, I went in and got Libby to come out and be polite. Everyone hugged and kissed and Mrs. and Mr. McKenzie thanked Libby and me and said they looked forward to seeing us at the Campbells'. And then they left.

I watched the carriage go back down the rise to the road with Mrs. Frederiksen standing beside me, her hand on my shoulder. Lib had already gone back in. I told Mrs. Frederiksen I was going to the barn to do evening chores.

Once I had the horses and Bessie in their stalls, I went to pet Flynn. He nickered and came to me, lifting his head over the fence to be patted.

"Are you a show horse?" I asked him, reaching up to push a tickly loose hair off my forehead.

He tossed his head, shooing flies, then nibbled at my hair.

"Do you know more tricks besides kneeling?" I asked, trying to smooth out the hair he had tousled. He bobbed his head again. I felt clammy and I swallowed hard. How many times had he seemed to know what I was saying, agreeing with me—or disagreeing? "You are a pretty horse," I said. He stood still. "Mrs. McKenzie seems very kind." He didn't move a muscle. "Are you handsome, like she said?" I asked, and he shook his head.

Nodding or shaking his head—what made the difference?

I asked him five more questions and he shook his head every time. Then he reached out to nibble my hair again. I patted him and leaned against his neck, then stood back, pushing my hair out of my eyes. "Do you know I really love you?"

He nodded.

And I blinked, realizing my hand was on my hair, still. I left it there. "Do you think you can win the race?" I asked him. He nodded.

I asked him three more questions, all three with my hands at my sides. He shook his head every time. Then I asked him if he was sure he could win the race, lifting my hand to pretend to scratch my ear. He nodded. It *was* a trick. I could imagine a crowd laughing.

I stared at Flynn. I had never heard about anyone who knew how to teach a horse to kneel or nod or anything like that. I still couldn't think of a single reason any farmer or rancher would take the time to do it—people worked dawn to dusk on their places just to keep the farms going. Maybe some rich man had made a hobby of learning how to train his horse to do tricks, but that seemed about as likely as snow in July. Mr. McKenzie had probably just missed the announcements.

I felt almost sick and I knew I had to tell someone, and I would. But not until after the race. Five days. Maybe the prize money wouldn't be enough to buy him—but maybe it would be. And it was my only hope.

CHAPTER TEN

❧ ❧ ❧

As Harvest Day got closer, Libby got quieter and grumpier. I had no idea what to do about it—I had never known how to cheer her up. I only knew how not to upset her even more. So I did my chores fast and well, then looked for ways to help her with her work.

I rode Flynn every day, galloping him for long stretches. His wind had improved, and he was getting faster, too. It seemed smart to be at one edge of the road or the other. There were wagon ruts down the middle—not deep, and the dirt was soft, but the shoulders of the road were flat. There were long curves in the road, too, and one day I realized the inside of every curve was shorter. I noticed something else, too. I had to hold Flynn back a little when Cory and I galloped. He was faster than Merry. I began to think that I really might have a chance.

Libby hated all the riding, I could tell, and I think she was a little hurt by how close Cory and I were getting. I didn't know what to do about that. I invited her to ride Tish and come with us, but of course she wouldn't. And she kept insisting that she wasn't going to come to Harvest Day.

One morning, Cory asked Joseph to ride with us and show us anything that might help one of us win the race. I didn't expect him to say yes, but he did. We galloped our usual two miles, with Joseph showing us ways to maneuver and how to pace our horses. Then we reined in and rode at a relaxed jog, letting the horses cool off.

Cory and I stopped at our usual place—about a half mile from the soddy—and started to say our good-byes. We only had two more days to ride together. Cory's father had told us both to let our horses rest the entire day before the race.

"Maybe we should ride you all the way home," Joseph said.

I started to tell him that there was no need to when I saw Cory trying not to laugh and I understood. He wanted to meet Libby.

"That would be lovely," I said, and Cory had to cover her mouth with one hand and turn away.

Joseph nodded, his lips pressed tight, ignoring us both.

I nudged Flynn and we led the way at an easy jog. I pulled back to a walk when we got to the path and they reined in, too. Cory made a funny little sound as we started up the rise and I refused to look at her. Joseph was her brother and he would love her no matter what. But if *I* laughed at him, he might not forgive me.

Libby was in the kitchen as usual, but Mrs. Frederiksen was on the porch. She looked up, and when she saw Joseph, she smiled. Had my mother been like her? Happy when something surprised her? I hoped so. And even if she hadn't been, that was how I wanted to be.

"Good morning," Joseph said. "It's good to see you, Mrs. Frederiksen."

She stood up. "You have become a man," she said, and I could see that pleased Joseph. He dismounted, smiling. I slid off Flynn and went to the doorway. Libby was straining curds. My coming in startled her and she frowned. There was a big pot of stew simmering on the hearth and she'd just laid wood on, so the fire was snapping and popping—she hadn't heard the hoofbeats.

"Cory and her brother are here."

She frowned again, and looked around, like she was looking for a way to get out.

"Just come meet them, please. Please, Libby. You like Cory, and Joseph is really nice, too."

I waited for her to refuse, but she didn't—probably because she couldn't. What reason could she possibly have not to come say hello? She splashed cold water on her face and lifted her apron to dry it. Then she undid the strings of her apron and took it off, smoothing her dress.

I went to the door and opened it, glancing back to make sure Libby was behind me. When I looked forward again, I found myself staring straight at Joseph. For an instant, he had a pleasant expression on his face, the kind of half smile people wear when they are being polite. I could tell the instant that he saw Lib. His face lit up.

"This is my sister, Libby," I said, and his eyes didn't so much as flicker toward my face. "Libby, this is Cory's older brother, Joseph."

He was smiling. Lib was blushing. I blush all the time, but Libby almost never did. And she was as pink as roses. Cory made the odd little sound again and I shot her a stern look. She took a deep breath, trying not to laugh at the way her brother was staring at my sister.

"I'll watch the stew," Mrs. Frederiksen said. Libby didn't answer beyond a vague nod. I gestured to Cory and she came up the porch steps and we followed Mrs. Frederiksen into the kitchen. I started to pull the door closed and Mrs. Frederiksen caught my eye. "Leave it open," she whispered close to my ear. "Libby looked pretty nervous. She might want to come back in."

I nodded and turned to look at the hearth. The stew was simmering. The kitchen was spotless. There was nothing to do. Cory was looking around. I looked at the wax paper covering the window. We'd had to replace it after the tornado and Mrs. Frederiksen hadn't had a piece quite big enough. There was a little gap along the bottom.

Cory smiled. "There's a soddy on our place. I was born in it, but I don't remember living there. After my parents had three children, Papa decided to build the house we live in now."

"I remember you as a little girl, chasing after your brothers," Mrs. Frederiksen said.

Cory swallowed and hesitated.

"Her younger brother passed away two years ago," I said quietly.

Mrs. Frederiksen nodded and reached out to touch Cory's shoulder. "My husband is buried east of the pasture and I miss him, too. It is a hard thing, losing someone you love."

Cory's eyes had flooded with tears and so had Mrs. Frederiksen's. I blinked, feeling my own eyes sting. For a long moment, we just stood there, not quite crying. Then Mrs. Frederiksen took my hand, and Cory's. Cory reached out and we completed the circle for an instant. Then, out on the porch, Libby laughed and startled us all. It wasn't a laugh so much as a too-high giggle. I heard Joseph's voice and she giggled again.

Mrs. Frederiksen sighed. "Isn't that just the way it always is?" she asked. "Tears and laughter. Both at once." She wiped her eyes on her apron and then gestured at Cory. "Want to see the rest of the place? It's just my little bedroom, a storeroom, and a hall so short if you blink you'll miss it." She took the lantern off the hook and led Cory along. I stayed in the kitchen, my feelings all in a tangle.

"This is where we hid from the tornado," I heard Mrs. Frederiksen saying, and I heard Cory ask a question. I moved toward the door. I could hear Libby and Joseph talking, but I was afraid to open the door to peek.

When Mrs. Frederiksen and Cory came back into the little kitchen, I asked Cory if she wanted to see the barn. She scrunched up her forehead and I jutted my chin toward the door to remind her that Libby and Joseph were out there.

"I love barns," Cory said.

Mrs. Frederiksen smiled, then leaned forward to whisper. "Don't tease them. Don't bother them at all unless Libby looks desperately uncomfortable."

We both promised. Then we went out. Joseph and Libby were talking, sitting on the steps. They didn't look up when we came out, so we climbed through the railing. I untied Flynn's reins, then we started down the path to the barn. I glanced back once. Libby looked up and saw me. I waved, but I am not sure she saw it. Joseph said something and she looked at him again.

"Do you think she'll come to the dance?" Cory asked.

I shrugged, sliding the rails back to put Flynn in the pasture. "I can't tell if she is enjoying talking to him or just too embarrassed to go back inside."

"Joseph is such a charmer," Cory told me. "He can make anyone at ease."

I looked out at the horses to hide my reaction. What if Libby really liked him? What if they wanted to get married one day? Somehow, I had never once thought about what that would mean for me.

It was very strange to think about living anywhere without Libby. But at least now, I knew I could stay here. Flynn came to the gate and nuzzled my cheek, then wandered off to graze.

"Mrs. Frederiksen is really nice," Cory said.

I nodded. "Your mother said everyone who knows her thinks well of her. I am sure it's true."

"It's only two more days, then Harvest Day," she said. I nodded and neither one of us said another word about it. We were both nervous. Cory was nervous about the race. So was I, but I was even more scared that I would find out who owned Flynn and lose him forever. And I was worried that Libby wouldn't come at all.

That evening, after supper, once Libby and I were snuggled under our blankets and staring at the hearth coals, I asked if she would come to the Campbells'. She nodded, but then she shook her head. "*No*. I don't know how to dance." She kept her voice low and I knew she didn't want Mrs. Frederiksen to hear.

"Joseph would teach you," I said softly.

"I think he is a very nice young man," she whispered. In the glow from the hearth, I couldn't see if she blushed, but I think she did.

"There will be a dozen or two of nice young men there," I whispered back. "Cory said he's a charmer." I wanted her to know, so her feelings wouldn't be hurt if their conversation hadn't meant as much to him as it had to her. But when I looked at Libby, I was sorry I had said it.

"You mean he acts like that with everyone?"

I bit my lip. "I don't know. Cory just said he's good at putting people at ease. That doesn't mean he doesn't like you a lot."

"I don't care," she said quietly. "I don't think we will be here for Harvest Day anyway."

"You're just saying that because you're scared," I said, and instantly wished I hadn't. I knew better than to start an argument when she was upset.

She turned over. "I really think it's best if we leave soon. I've been saying it for a long time and then you found the horse, so I let it go. But I think it's time."

"Libby, I really—"

"We're leaving," she repeated. "We've been here too long as it is."

I started to remind her how hard I had been working to get Flynn ready for the race, how Mrs. Frederiksen's daughter was hoping we would stay—but I knew there was almost no chance of her listening. Not now. And I knew something else, too. She might wake me up before dawn, and she would have all our things tied up in bundles and be ready to leave.

I was quiet a long time, then my anger won out. "I don't want to go," I said, turning over to look at the ceiling.

"It's that horse," she hissed.

"You know how hard I've worked to try to win the race, how much I have always wanted a horse."

"We can't take it with us even if you win and buy it."

"But if we stay here it would—" I began.

"We aren't staying," she interrupted.

"The race is day after *tomorrow*—" I began.

"And we won't be here," she interrupted.

I lay still, trying to think of something to say, something that would convince her. But there wasn't anything, and I knew it. I lay in the darkness a long time, trying to think of a way to make Libby understand what I knew in my heart.

This was as close to a real home as we might ever have.

Mrs. Frederiksen loved us.

And I loved her.

CHAPTER ELEVEN

❧ ❧ ❧

I woke the next morning knowing what I had to do. But I couldn't make myself do it. So I left the house early, barely speaking to Libby. I rode Flynn, just jogging him a little, riding just far enough to feel alone with my thoughts. They were blowing every which way. I thought about asking Joseph to come talk to her, but that was wrong and I knew it. He might like her a lot, eventually. He barely knew her now. I thought about hiding all my clothes—and hers—so she wouldn't be able to pack up. I thought about waiting until she was asleep, then going to sleep in the barn, where she couldn't find me. But I knew all of that was silly and wouldn't solve anything.

When we got back, I put Flynn in the pasture, then finished my barn chores. I mucked the stalls and sat with Flynn a long time, then I went up to the house. I saw Mrs. Frederiksen in the garden and I longed to go help her hoe weeds, to do anything but talk to Libby. I was scared in a deep, strange way that made my whole body feel weak. But I had no choice.

I walked into the kitchen and waited until Libby turned to look at me. "Have you decided to stay here?" I asked her.

She shook her head. "No. We're leaving tonight."

I took a deep breath and tried to say it, but nothing came out.

Libby gaped her mouth and then laughed. "You look like a fish, Margret." She shook her head. "I have work to do. I want to leave here with all our clothes clean and—"

"I'm not going with you," I said.

I meant to make my voice firm and clear, but it came out a raspy whisper and I knew from the expression on her face that she hadn't understood me. "I'm not going with you," I repeated.

Before Libby had a chance to respond, Mrs. Frederiksen put her head in the door. "Margret, could you help me with something for a while?"

"No, she can't!" Libby snapped. "Don't we do enough around here?"

I turned to face Mrs. Frederiksen. "May I just talk to my sister first?"

She glanced past me at Libby, then looked into my eyes. "Of course. I won't come in again until one of you calls me." Then she was gone.

I turned back and met Libby's eyes. Her face was hard now and that made me angrier than anything else, for some reason. "She is always kind to you," I said. "Always. How dare you talk to her like that?"

Lib didn't answer, she just glared at me.

"Last night I wanted to talk you into going to the dance," I said. "I wanted you to see me race, but now I'm glad you won't be there."

"Neither will you," she said quietly.

I stood up taller. "You can't make me leave. I am not a two-year-old anymore, Libby. You can't just pick me up and—"

"Be quiet!" she shouted, and I saw a wild, scared look in her eyes that I had never seen before. Before I even knew I was turning, I was out the door, my heart thudding. I ran to the barn, skidding and sliding as I turned the corner to go in the wide doors.

I stood in Flynn's stall and I leaned against his neck and I cried longer than I had ever cried in my life. And I learned something. Libby was wrong.

Crying did help. If you cry long enough, you don't feel worse, you feel a little better. Nothing goes away, of course; I still had to stand up to my sister. But when I did go back up the path, I felt steadier, stronger.

Mrs. Frederiksen was in the garden still. She was pulling weeds, facing away from me. When I went back into the soddy, Libby had her back to me, too. She was sitting at the table, the soap grater and a dish before her, but she was just sitting, looking at the wall.

"No," I said, "I won't be quiet."

She turned to stare at me. I went and pulled out the chair opposite hers. "I like it here and I am going to stay, Libby."

She shook her head. "She'll turn you out the day her daughter talks her into moving into Denver City. Then you won't have anywhere to go and I will be long gone and—"

"She loves us," I began, but Libby smacked the table with her right hand.

"*You*, maybe. Not me." She glared at me, her eyes glassy with tears. "She thinks I am mean to you and I know I am sometimes, but ever since that first night . . ."

I knew instantly what night she meant and I was dumbstruck. Not a single word formed in my throat. She had never talked to me about this. Never. Not a single word and I just stared at her, holding my breath.

Libby rocked back and forth a few times, then she cleared her throat. "We made it to that farmhouse and the woman said—" Libby cleared her throat again and fell silent for a long moment, then started over. "I don't remember why, but Papa had the team whipped up into a gallop. There were rocks the size of houses along the road. I remember that. And I remember Mother screaming, holding on to us so tight that her nails left marks." She rubbed her arm, staring at the wall as she went on. "One of the horses stumbled and they both went down. The carriage tipped and slid and smashed into the rocks." She touched her face. "I remember being all skinned up. You were off to one side, on the ground, crying. I was trying to quiet you when three men rode up. They had seen the carriage go over, I guess. They pulled Papa free of the wreck. Then Mama. Neither of them moved, Margret. And I knew. I *knew*."

Libby wiped at her eyes. "The men said they would take us somewhere safe. I didn't want to leave, but they put us on their horses and rode. I screamed and screamed, but the man held me tight and kept saying everything would be all right."

Libby took a long shuddery breath, then went on. "It was a farmhouse. They were very kind to us, took care of us. But I heard them talking, calling us 'poor little orphans.' But they wanted to keep you," she said. "Not me. They thought maybe the miller would take me, if I could be taught to sew flour sacks." She stopped for a few seconds, and I held my breath. Then she finished. "We left that night. It wasn't too cold and I stole the blanket."

She looked at me and I saw streams of tears were running down her cheeks. "You were so little and maybe I should have left you there, but . . . I have done my best, Margret. I have."

"I know," I said. "And you saved us both."

She lowered her head and cried harder. I reached out and took her hand and she didn't push me away for a long time. And when she did, I got her a warm washcloth and sat back down. She pressed it to her face for so long that her cheeks were pink when she finally lowered it.

"I can help now," I said. "I can help decide things, Libby."

"I do want to go," she said, and somehow I knew she didn't mean leaving.

"To the dance?"

She nodded. "I am so scared," she whispered. "What if Joseph doesn't talk to me at all? What if they can all tell that we aren't—" She stopped as though there was no word for what she meant.

"Like them?"

She nodded.

"I don't feel too different around Cory," I told her. "We are alike more than we are different—horses and riding and chores. It'll be like that for you."

"Papa loved horses," Libby said. "He was off training horses for the army when you were born. It was just Mama and me and the midwife." She looked at me. "That was during the War Between the States."

And that pushed us both into another long silence. I wanted to hear everything she remembered about our parents. But it wasn't the most important thing to me anymore. She was.

"I'm scared to go, too," I said. "That's part of why I want you to come."

Libby looked at me for so long that I thought maybe all the talk and all the tears hadn't changed anything. But she finally took a long breath and said, "Then I will." And then she said this: "And we can stay here, if she will have us." She wiped her eyes and sniffled. "For a while longer, anyway. We can decide later, can't we?"

I nodded, holding my breath. I felt my eyes stinging. I wasn't going to lose my sister after all. And my love of horses had come from our father? The idea made my heart lift.

"Maybe you should call Mrs. Frederiksen in," Libby said quietly. "She's been out there a long time."

I walked out to the garden and told Mrs. Frederiksen that Libby and I had decided to stay, at least for now, if that was all right, and that Lib had said she would go to the Campbells'. Mrs. Frederiksen held me for a moment, then stepped back. "I am very glad to have you stay. Both of you, as long as you like. We should talk about it more, the three of us. Tell her that. I'll just finish weeding, then I'll come in."

I went back up the path. Libby had the flour sack open and the butter crock out. While I spoke she was beating eggs to make a cake. "Mrs. Frederiksen said we were to bring a dessert," she said quietly, "and I—" She gestured at the kitchen. "I always feel better doing something and we aren't ready to go at all." She looked at me. "If I forbid you to ride in the race—"

"You can't," I said quietly. "I have to ride in it, Libby." I spoke softly, because she had sounded almost wistful, not mean, or angry, or bossy.

She exhaled and stared into my eyes. Then she nodded, a tiny motion. "All right. I hate it, but I guess there's no stopping you."

We were both quiet for a long moment, just looking at each other. Then she nodded again. "Will you grate soap for laundry?"

I smiled at her and set to work. By the time Mrs. Frederiksen came in, the sun was slanting low in the windows and we were rinsing out our best dresses while the bathwater was heating up.

Mrs. Frederiksen took the first bath this time. Then she lit two lanterns and went into her room. "Call me when you are finished," she said, then closed her door. Lib and I scrubbed hard, trying to get every bit of everyday dirt off, then we dressed in our nightgowns, shivering a little when we carried the tub out onto the porch to dump the water. The sun wasn't quite down yet, but it wouldn't be long.

Once we had the kitchen cleaned up, we stood looking at each other for a long moment. "It will be all right," I told her. And I tried to say it the way she had always said it to me—like I was sure.

She nodded.

Then I called to Mrs. Frederiksen.

"Let me show you something," she called back. "Both of you. Come see what I found."

Lib followed me down the little hall. The lanterns were hung on opposite sides of the room. Mrs. Frederiksen's trunk stood open and there was a mound of clothing on her bed. The room was heavy with the smell of mint and tansy and something else I didn't recognize until I saw the reddish wood on the underside of the trunk's lid. Cedar.

"I have been an old woman a long time," Mrs. Frederiksen said. "I put in fresh herbs spring and fall to keep the moths off, but I had nearly forgotten most of what was in there." She smoothed her hair and blinked a few times, and I knew she had found memories as well as old clothes. "We are a weepy bunch of women this week, aren't we?" she said.

I glanced at Libby. She *smiled*.

Mrs. Frederiksen motioned for us to stand at the foot of the bed. Then she held up a dress. I heard Libby inhale sharply. I could only stare. "It's far too fancy for the picnic and the games, Libby," Mrs. Frederiksen said. "You'll want to wear your good gingham dress for the day, the race and all. But then you can change into this for the dance."

I stared. The cloth, even creased and wrinkled from years in the trunk, still shone softly. It was blue, summer-dawn blue. The sleeves were slender and long, cuffed in lace. "I wore it to a friend's wedding," Mrs. Frederiksen said. "In Philadelphia, before we ever thought of coming west." She pulled at the cloth and shook it out a few times. "Silk never wears out, if you can keep the bugs off."

Silk?

I heard Libby make a tiny sound and I glanced at her. Her eyes were closed. "Mama had a silk dress. It was—"

"Green," I said, speaking before I lost the tiny wisp of a memory that had come out of nowhere. For an instant I saw her, a memory as clear as creek water, wearing a deep green gown, the same kind of shining, slippery cloth. I saw my mother. It took my breath away.

I looked up at Mrs. Frederiksen, about to explain, then I didn't, because she was already smiling, a look of pure joy on her face, and I knew she understood.

Libby washed the dress in warm water, with vinegar and a little grated soap. She hung it over the backs of two blanket-draped chairs, smoothing the fabric gently every few minutes until the wrinkles were gone. Then we all went to bed.

CHAPTER TWELVE

❧ ❧ ❧

*L*ibby had ironed the silk dress. After I washed and dried my hands, she let me touch it. The cloth slid like water over my skin. "It fits like it was made for me," she said. Then she shook her head. "Mrs. Frederiksen has been showing me how to dance. I should have started sooner." She smiled a little, but her voice was quivery.

"You have a knack," Mrs. Frederiksen called down the hallway. "The music will teach you the rest."

"Did Mama and Papa dance?" I asked, hoping they had, that she had gotten the knack from them the way I had gotten my trust in horses.

She closed her eyes and thought about it. "I don't know. Maybe. She had dress-up clothes and they would go into St. Louis sometimes, and leave us with a woman named Neva."

Neva. *St. Louis?* I had a thousand questions and didn't let myself ask even one of them. Libby's eyes were full of pain and she was shaking her head. "I am so nervous I could barely sleep last night."

"Me, too," I told her.

The sun was almost up. Lib packed the cake in a wooden cracker box. Mrs. Frederiksen picked a crateful of sweet corn. I hitched Tish and Bennie to the wagon, then drove them up the hill. While Lib and Mrs. Frederiksen loaded the wagon, I ran down to the barn and gave Flynn the brushing of his life. Not a speck of dust was on him and his mane and tail were combed out so that they almost floated on the morning breeze.

Then we all washed up and got dressed. Lib didn't braid her hair and it was beautiful hanging over her shoulders and down her back. I braided mine and I wore my work dress—the one I always wore riding—I would change after the race. The silk dress, enclosed in a bedsheet, went on top of everything else in the wagon bed, and it was the first thing we unloaded once we got there.

Mrs. Campbell laid it out on Cory's bed, then stood back, staring at it.

"You forget what a good dress looks like out here," she said, turning to Mrs. Frederiksen. They exchanged a long look and I remembered that both of them had grown up back east.

"You are so pretty," Mrs. Campbell said to Libby. "And wearing this? I hope you like to dance. I don't think you will be sitting down very much tonight." Lib blushed and ducked her head, but I could see she was smiling.

When we walked back down, there were two more wagons in the yard and I could see three coming up the road. Joseph had appeared from whatever work his father had had him doing. Now he was pointing, guiding people to the long rows of elms where they could tether their wagons and saddle horses in the shade. I happened to be looking at him when he half turned and saw us. Or saw Libby, anyway. He stared for a few seconds, then someone shouted and he had to look away.

The Campbells had thought of everything. For the dance, there was a huge patch of level ground that had been weeded, then raked, then swept—with the wooden platform at one end for the musicians. For the picnic, there were flat sawn sections of logs, just the right size for stools, where people could sit and eat. There were eight or ten planked tables, with benches for anyone who wanted to sit and eat more slowly and spend some time talking to their neighbors. Cory said the tables and the logs had been brought in two or three wagonloads, a few months apart over the year, from the Johnsons' place—where Harvest Day had been held the year before.

The whole thing amazed me—how much work everyone had gone to, how the women had made sure, among themselves, that enough meat was brought, enough bread, enough pies and cakes. The older girls were all dressed up, but I scanned the crowd, and no one was as beautiful as my sister—not even close.

I saw the McKenzies. Caleb and Ruth came running up to me to wish me luck in the race. I hugged them both and thanked them, then went to chat with their parents for a moment. Mrs. McKenzie seemed to know everyone there and I wondered if I would come back to Harvest Day ten or fifteen years from now, to see old friends again.

If it hadn't been for worrying over the race, it would have been the best day of my whole life.

Cory and I won the three-legged race and she played six rounds of checkers before anyone beat her—she won over grown men with gray hair and forty more years of checker games to their credit. Libby was standing off to one side for a long time, next to Mrs. Frederiksen. Then, when I looked up, she was gone. I caught Mrs. Frederiksen's eye and she nodded toward the house. I turned and saw Libby following Joseph across the lawn, both of them carrying pies. I looked back to smile at Mrs. Frederiksen, but she was embracing a gray-haired man, both of them grinning. He sat with us when we ate—they had known each other more than twenty years and it was fun to listen to them talk about Littleton when it had been two wagon ruts leading to the ford across the river.

I kept running out to the line of trees to check Flynn. Coming back the third time, I cut across the pasture and ended up walking by another line of elms that separated the house yard from the barnyard. There were no wagons there, just saddle horses. I sprinted, hurrying to get back in time to find Cory before the picnic started. The last horse in the row shied at the sound of my footfalls, jerking back so hard that I stumbled to a halt, talking to her in a soft voice, moving out from behind her and around the end of the row so she could see me clearly.

It was a pretty bay mare, her eyes rimmed in white, "I apologize," I told her. "I sure didn't meant to startle you like that. You all right now?" She shook her mane and I stared at her, remembering her fine-boned face. I stepped to one side so that the sunlight slanted across her flanks. I exhaled, glancing toward the house, then behind me. So the cowboy was here somewhere and maybe Flynn did belong to him—the mare seemed to know the same trick. The idea made me feel sick. The welt marks weren't fresh now, but the whipping had left scars that were still visible beneath her shining coat. "Do you know Flynn?" I asked the mare, making sure to bring my voice up at the end of the sentence. She shook her head again. I bit my lip, then tried it once more with my hand on my hair. She nodded, ducking her head and tossing her mane.

Uncertain what to do, I went back to find Cory and spotted her weaving through the crowd, looking for me. "The starting-line judges rode out about ten minutes ago. We're supposed to ride up there now," she said. She smiled at me and held out her hand. "If I don't win, I hope you do." I smiled back at her as we shook hands. "My father says it'd be good to jog them up there, no galloping, no walking," she added.

Then we separated, her running for the barn, and me heading back to the line of elm trees. I was out of breath when I got to Flynn. He was happy to see me, as always. He nuzzled my hair before I swung up. Then I stared toward the road. Somehow, I had to get Flynn past the crowd without the cowboy noticing him. Eli. Had he spotted me already? I knew I hadn't seen him—I would have recognized him instantly.

A few of the other riders were starting off and I could see two men setting up a white pole beside the road just past the Campbells' lane. The crowd would soon walk down there, everyone finding a place to watch near the finish line. For now, the crowd was still scattered. People were laughing, standing in loose circles to talk. There were men at the horseshoe pits. I scanned the faces, looking for the cowboy, not sure I could spot him from this far off. But if he was here looking for Flynn, he wouldn't have any trouble seeing him as I rode down the lane, then up the road. I noticed a man walking toward me. My stomach clenched, but he angled off to check a tethered wagon team.

I saw Cory riding up the lane and I nudged Flynn into a canter along the row of horses and wagons, all the way to the front fence, reining in beside Cory so that as we turned on to the road, Flynn was on the outside, shielded by Merry from anyone watching.

I held my breath. No one shouted. I kept glancing at the crowd as we jogged away. I couldn't see anyone staring, noticing us at all, except Lib and Mrs. Frederiksen, both of them blowing kisses. Cory and I waved back. Then three other riders came out of the gate behind us, and then a few more, and then we were far enough away that I exhaled. Then I glanced up the road and saw a man standing way off to the side, alone, staring at the horses. No, not all the horses. At Flynn. But it wasn't the cowboy. He was just looking because Flynn was such a good horse, I told myself. He didn't call out or come toward us, and I let out another long breath.

"Are you all right?" Cory asked me.

"Just nervous about the race, about someone seeing Flynn."

She reached out and took my hand and we rode that way for a while, holding hands. Then a few of the riders cantered up behind us and loped past. They got half a mile ahead or so, then reined back in.

"Why would they do that?" I asked Cory.

"Maybe they want to line up first. But my father said to hold Merry to a jog."

And so I held Flynn in, too, and hoped that her father was right. I looked ahead, then back. There were fifteen riders, counting Cory and me. I saw only four grown men—the rest were boys and three of them were riding bareback. Flynn stayed at a jog, but he knew something was coming up, I could tell. As we got close to the starting line, I saw the riders who had passed us sitting their horses in disorganized groups, waiting. Then I heard the judges shouting to get everyone's attention. Cory caught my eye and mouthed, "Good luck." I said it back to her, and then a man shouted.

"Line 'em up!"

I leaned forward and galloped Flynn to the line, staying so far to the edge of the road that when I reined in and turned him back, I was exactly where I wanted to be. A man with a dark cowboy hat rode around me, then cleared his throat like I was supposed to move over. I pretended not to hear him, rubbing Flynn's neck and combing his mane with my fingers. The man finally spat on the ground and turned a small circle, bringing his horse up between me and the next rider. Good. We had the outside spot.

"Little girls oughtn't ride in horse races," the man said, keeping his voice low.

I have no idea what got into me, but I looked at him instead of looking down. "We'll see, won't we, sir?" I said politely.

"Rideeeeers readyyyyyyy?" came the shout from a man holding a willow switch with a red kerchief tied on the end like a flag.

I nodded along with the others.

"Anyone who starts before I lower the flag will be disqualified at the end of the race," he shouted. "Judges ready?"

Two men at either side of the line shouted back. I fixed my eyes on the flag and tightened my legs against Flynn's sides. I felt him tense.

"Ready, set . . . go!" the flagman shouted, and swooped the flag downward on the last word. I dug my bare heels into Flynn's sides, but he had heard the word *go* and he was already leaping forward.

CHAPTER THIRTEEN

※ ※ ※

*T*he sudden thunder of the hoofbeats startled me, but as Flynn hurled himself forward, I sat tight, just making sure I stayed on his back. I gave him his head; then, as he settled into his stride, I glanced down the line—we were already ahead of more than half the horses. I moved my weight forward as Flynn hit his rhythm, riding up close to his withers, leaning forward over his neck when he sprang off his back legs, settling my weight just a little when his forehooves hit, then leaning forward again. I did it without thinking. We had practiced so much that it was as natural to me as making sure my weight was balanced above my own legs when I ran.

On our left, the man who had chided me was already whipping his horse with the ends of his reins. To do that, he had to sit up straighter, which slowed his horse just enough for Flynn to be almost a length ahead after twenty or so strides. So I shortened the left rein half an inch and Flynn responded, galloping at an angle so slight the man beside me didn't see what I was doing, then cursed when he noticed that we had moved in front of him.

I glanced across the line again. There were two horses ahead of us by half a stride. One was Cory, the other one of the boys about my age. His horse was hammerheaded, a dull roan, but it had a wondrous long stride and the boy knew how to ride. I put my eyes back on the road ahead and sat light as a feather.

What I wanted was to let Flynn pace himself, to run like he didn't have me on his back at all. I knew he wouldn't drop behind if I let him alone—he never had with Merry. We came to the first curve and I moved Flynn over just a little again, taking advantage of the inside curve to gain just a little more distance, then I let him run his own course again. I glanced at Cory. Merry was galloping easily and Cory looked steady and determined.

It was at the next curve that the boy on the roan began to pull away from the rest of us. Flynn put on speed to keep up and I let him, at first, then it scared me, going so fast this soon. Could the roan really run the whole distance that hard? If he could, and we got very far behind, Flynn would never be able to catch up. But if he couldn't, Flynn might wear down too soon and lose to someone with a fresher horse at the finish line.

I watched the roan for a full minute before I decided. He was galloping fast, his neck extended, and he was working hard—his nostrils were flared and nothing about his stride looked easy or smooth. I was pretty sure he couldn't keep it up. So I pulled Flynn back, just a little at a time, like the roan was beating us, like Flynn couldn't keep up. I glanced back and Cory met my eyes for an instant and I was pretty sure she was doing what I was—holding Merry back for the same reason. I kept Flynn steady and we stayed a length or two behind the roan as the ground blurred beneath his hooves and the first mile of the race slid past.

Then, suddenly, the man in the dark hat whipped his horse up beside me and, an inch at a time, veered so that he was edging Flynn to the outside. I shouted at him, but he pretended not to hear me. Scared, I looked down the road. There was so little room I was afraid to urge Flynn faster, scared that I wouldn't make it and we'd end up galloping headlong over the rough ground—no race was worth hurting Flynn.

So I reined Flynn in, letting the man in the dark hat take the lead as I dropped back into the tangle of riders behind us. I was furious, mostly with myself. If I hadn't been rude, he might not have done it. Because I had let my temper show, Flynn could have been hurt, and now we might lose the race.

Flynn pulled at the tightened reins and I held him in, trying to think. We were still a mile from the finish line. The slowest horses had dropped farther back, then there was a group not far behind me—and four of us were more or less in the lead, riding close together—Cory and the boy on the roan were two lengths out in front, then the man in the dark hat riding on the edge of the road, then Flynn and me.

Flynn pulled at the reins again and I let him out, moving him a little toward the center of the road, into a clearer position, but still behind the man in the dark hat. I wanted to get away from him altogether, but angling Flynn all the way to the other side of the road would take too long and it would be dangerous—for everyone. The man glanced back and moved in front of us again. So I just held Flynn back and waited. The man in the dark hat had no idea how strong Flynn was—and by the time he realized it, it would be too late.

When there was a half mile to go, I brought my weight farther forward and felt Flynn gather himself. Then I reined him to the left, let out the reins, and dug my bare heels into his sides. Flynn leaped forward, lengthening his stride. It felt like he was as angry at the man in the dark hat as I was. We came up beside him so fast that he jerked around to stare at me, then whipped at his horse's flanks again. I glanced back at him every few seconds until I was sure he wasn't gaining ground, he was losing it. Then I looked down the road again. Cory and the boy on the roan were moving faster and faster, running almost neck and neck.

Flynn pounded after them, digging into the dirt with his forehooves and coming off his hind-quarters like he was jumping over hot coals with every stride. I held still, concentrating on staying with him, trying to ride light as a feather.

The boy on the roan had moved ahead of Cory and was galloping straight down the middle of the road. He wasn't whipping his horse—the roan wanted to win on his own, but his ears were back and his nostrils were wide and there was sweat-foam on his shoulders. He was tiring. I angled Flynn slightly, getting him back on the smooth dirt at the edge of the road, well ahead of the man in the dark hat now. Then I looked straight ahead and leaned forward, squeezing my legs against Flynn's sides and willing him to win. He didn't hesitate and he didn't falter, he flattened out, giving every bit of his strength when I asked him to.

On opposite sides of the road, Cory and I galloped almost in unison for a dozen strides, then Flynn began to inch ahead. Cory and Merry dropped back a little, then a little more. Smooth and strong, Flynn gained with every stride and soon only the roan was between us and the finish line.

The crowd had gathered on both sides of the road ahead. I could just hear their shouts over the sound of hoofbeats. Stride by stride, Flynn caught up to the roan and passed him. Then we were flying over the ground, people on both sides of the road, cheering. I saw the finish pole and heard the cheers rise, even louder, and then we were past it all, still galloping down the empty road, just Flynn and me, all alone.

I had a hard time pulling Flynn in. He slowed, and I knew he was tired, but he didn't want to stop. When I finally managed to get him in hand, we were a half mile past the finish line. I pulled him to a canter, then a trot, then, finally, to a weary walk. And I thought, for an instant, about not going back. I reined in and stared up the road for a long time.

Then I heard hoofbeats and I turned to see Cory cantering toward me. She was grinning. "You did it!" she shouted, then whooped. I smiled at her. If she was upset over losing, she was kind enough to hide it so I could enjoy winning. I blew her a kiss and she laughed. Then, as she got closer, she called out, "Come on! Everyone is waiting to cheer you." She shook her head. "And I wasn't the only one who saw what that man did. He's not a neighbor—he's someone's cousin from Denver City or something. Whoever he is, he'll never be allowed to race here again."

I nodded and looked down road once more before I turned Flynn around and started back. Cory rode beside me. She was talking about the race, how all the men were astounded at how well I rode, what a fine horse Flynn was. I tried to listen to her, then to smile at the people calling out congratulations to me when we got closer. I wanted to be happy, and I loved Cory for being so happy for me, but I couldn't stop scanning the roadside crowd for the cowboy. I knew he was there somewhere, he had to be. But I didn't see him.

I reined in at the finish line and accepted the little leather pouch with thirty dollars in it—thirty! Then I smiled and waved when everyone clapped and shouted and whistled. I waved at Mrs. Frederiksen and Libby, both of them cheering, their hands cupped around their mouths.

Then, as Cory and I turned off the road and started down the lane, I saw the man I had noticed before and this time I knew he was looking at Flynn. When he beckoned to me to come closer, I realized, suddenly, maybe all this did make sense. Eli wasn't here and he wasn't the owner. He had stolen both Flynn and the bay mare from this man. Or maybe Flynn belonged to someone else. Or—

Cory reached out to touch my shoulder. "Margret?"

I gestured at the man standing in the pasture, waiting for me. "I think that might be Flynn's real owner." Saying it hurt.

Her smiled faded. "Do you want me to come, too? Should I get my father?"

I shook my head. There was nothing her father could do to help me. "But will you please tell Mrs. Frederiksen and Libby that I will come quick as I can?"

Cory nodded and I could see how worried she was, but she rode off and left me to face the man alone—which is how I wanted it. As I turned Flynn on to the grass, I was hoping that I was wrong and that he just wanted to admire Flynn or maybe try to buy him from me. But then Flynn suddenly lifted his head and whinnied. The man laughed and came forward just as Flynn pulled the reins looser so he could trot to meet him halfway.

I sat still, staring as Flynn nuzzled the man's face, then rested his muzzle on his shoulder while the man scratched his ears. When the man finally looked up at me, I expected him to curse me or accuse me of stealing his horse or something awful, but what he said was this:

"I am forever grateful to you. I cannot thank you enough for taking such good care of him."

I blinked and felt my eyes stinging as the man went on. "He's fit and sound and I can tell he has been loved." Then he laughed again as Flynn nudged his shoulder. "I didn't know he was that fast. I raised him from a colt." He rubbed Flynn's forehead and looked up at me. "Did he teach you any of his tricks?"

I tried to smile. "Kneeling and answering questions."

The man grinned. "He has many more. Jack is the smartest horse I have ever met." And then he told me about his equestrian show. He said they traveled all over, giving performances—and the audiences always loved Jack. "And Jack loves them," the man added, and smiled again. "I know the thief who stole him lost him in a storm. How did you find him?"

I slid off Flynn's back, and instantly wished I had stayed on him. I felt small, standing next to his owner. Small and sad. I told him the story, all of it, including the cowboy, and how Mrs. Frederiksen had protected Flynn. "We thought he was trying to steal any strays anyone had found."

"That was Eli Wates. The sheriff in Denver has him now. He stole two horses from me." The man shook his head. "Your Mrs. Frederiksen was right about him."

I explained why I had entered the race. "And I have thirty dollars," I said, extending the leather sack. "I have been hoping you might sell him to me."

He shook his head again. "I'm sorry," he said, and I could tell that he meant it. "I can't part with him. He's the best horse in my show, but even more than that, it would feel like letting someone walk away with my brother, almost."

I had taken a deep breath, intending to argue, politely, to try to convince him. But when he said that, I let it out slowly and didn't say another word. I knew exactly what he meant. And Flynn loved him, it was plain as day. *Jack*. My Flynn was really named Jack.

"I apologize for my manners, Miss—?"

"Quinn," I told him. "Margret Quinn."

He kept scratching Flynn's ears. "My name is Tom Richards. Are your parents here? I would like to thank them as well and pay them back whatever it has cost to feed Jack all this time."

I kept my chin up. At least now I had something to say. "My father was a horse trainer in St. Louis," I said, "but my sister and I are orphans. We're staying with Mrs. Frederiksen, up the road." I gestured. "I can pay her for the feed, now." I took a deep breath. "I have really gotten fond of your horse." I meant to say more, but I started to cry.

After a minute or two, I wiped my eyes and looked up. Mr. Richards put his hand on my shoulder. "Listen. If you don't have parents, I think you've already had your share of hard times. I don't want to add to them. Maybe we could work out a deal, you and I."

I wiped my eyes again, waiting for him to tell me he would let me come see Flynn in the show for free or something like that. Flynn sidled closer to me and nibbled at my hair. My eyes filled up again. I rubbed my sleeve across my face.

Mr. Richards squeezed my shoulder. "I have a bay mare—Jack's sister."

"I saw her," I said, gesturing to where the mare was tethered. "I thought the cowboy was here and I was afraid he really was Flynn's owner. I mean Jack's," I added, then wiped my eyes again. "She knows the answering trick, too."

Mr. Richards nodded and smiled. "She does, but she is so skittish now, I can't use her in the show. The crowds scare her." He kicked at the dirt. "Eli Wates beat her. She is the sweetest horse I ever raised and I can't imagine why he would hurt her." He was quiet a moment, then looked at me again. "We just finished a week of shows in Denver. Everyone else is on the way to Kansas City," he said. "I stayed behind, looking for Jack, and spotted the mare tied outside a Denver saloon." He paused. "With whip welts all over her sides."

He fell silent again, then looked up. "I rode out here because Wates claimed to have lost my horse in the storm, about five miles east of here. The man at the flour mill told me about the race, how almost everybody in the whole valley would be here. I hoped maybe someone might have seen Jack. But I didn't expect it to be someone like you." He smiled and patted Flynn again. "The mare needs a home, a good home with someone she could learn to trust."

It took me a long moment to understand what he was saying to me. "She's beautiful," I said carefully, my heart rising a little.

Mr. Richards nodded. "She is. And Sarah is one of the gentlest horses I have ever bred. And she is as smart as her brother." He patted Jack's neck.

"And I could have her?" I asked quietly, scared that I had misunderstood him. "Is that what you are saying? For my own?"

Mr. Richards nodded. "I will sell her to you so it's legal and binding. Does two dollars sound all right?"

I nodded, knowing that I would miss Flynn forever, but so happy that Mr. Richards would trust me with Sarah. Flynn would be happy—he was going home. And I would have my own horse!

"I should ask Mrs. Frederiksen," I said. "My sister and I are staying with her."

He nodded. "Go find two adults as witnesses. While you do that, I'll go switch my saddle to Jack. I'll meet you where Sarah is tethered?"

I nodded, staring at him. Then I whirled and ran.

It took less than a minute to find Mrs. Frederiksen. She was standing with Cory and

Libby—they had all been watching from a little ways off, worried when they had seen me crying. I explained everything and Mrs. Frederiksen hugged me, then Cory did. I almost started crying again. I faced Libby. "I'll take care of her. I know you never wanted me to have a horse, but—"

"You earned the mare," she said quietly. "I am just scared of horses because . . ."

And when she didn't finish, I nodded, to let her know that I finally understood. I might not remember the horses pounding along, the carriage crashing into the rocks, but she did.

I explained what Mr. Richards had said about needing witnesses. "Cory, will you ask your father to join us?" Mrs. Frederiksen asked. Cory nodded and took off at a run. "After we get your bill of sale," Mrs. Frederiksen said, "then you and Libby can go get changed for the dance." She tilted her head slightly, toward my sister. I nodded, understanding her. My fears were settled, for worse—and for better. But Libby had been waiting all day to face her own and she was as scared and nervous as I had been. Maybe worse.

Mr. Richards signed the paper and had me write my name, then Mrs. Frederiksen and Cory's father signed as witnesses.

"I have to be back in Denver City for the horse thief's trial in a month," he said. "Would you mind if I came to see Sarah then?"

"We would be pleased to have you," Mrs. Frederiksen said.

I stood, listening, looking at Sarah. She was watching us, wary, as though she thought one of us might try to hurt her. I understood her perfectly. She was like me, and even more like Libby. But she would learn, I was sure of it. I would never be cruel to her, and I would be careful not to startle her. With time, I was sure she would be all right.

I stepped away from everyone and went to stand by her. She was nervous when I touched her, but then she smelled me all over, the way horses always do with a stranger. I touched her neck lightly, then realized that Mr. Richards was saying good-bye. So I thanked him again—and he promised he would see us in a month. I patted Flynn and hugged his neck, my eyes stinging. Then I watched Mr. Richards mount and ride away.

I was staring after him when we heard the sound of a fiddler tuning up. Mrs. Frederiksen, Cory, and Libby started off.

"I have to go," I told Sarah. "But I'll be back, and we'll all go home together." I stood with her a moment more, patting her neck, then I ran to catch up.

Every room at the Campbells' was being used as a ladies' changing room. Cory and I and Libby—and Mrs. Frederiksen—used Cory's bedroom, taking turns doing up one another's hooks and buttons. Cory and I tied each other's hair ribbons and made sure our sashes were tied in nice, full bows. When I turned around, I saw Libby and caught my breath. Mrs. Frederiksen was brushing out her hair, both of them facing a long narrow mirror on the wall.

"Is that really me?" Libby whispered.

"Yes," we all said in unison, and she blushed. Then she stepped aside and I caught my breath a second time. Mrs. Frederiksen had found herself a dress in the trunk as well. Hers was a slender drape of deep brown fabric. And she had pinned her hair up higher on her head, twisted into coils where a crown would rest.

"You look like a queen and Libby looks like a princess," Mrs. Campbell said from the doorway. We all turned to laugh, then we made our way through the crowded hall and went to stand for a few minutes on the porch. The sun wasn't down yet, but it was getting low. There were lanterns hung from poles around the edge of the swept-earth dance floor, already lit.

"You really do look beautiful," I told Libby. She reached out and took my hand and held it tight for a long time. She only let go when she saw Joseph making his way toward her through the crowd just as the fiddle player began a tune, simple and sweet and not too fast.

Cory's father came and asked her to dance and she laughed and curtsied as he led her away. Several couples walked out and began a square. In time with the music, the men twirled their wives around, then held them close for a few steps, then turned again, the women flaring their skirts.

I looked back and saw Joseph talking to Libby. She was shaking her head, smiling, but he had her hand, and he gently pulled her forward. I crossed my fingers and watched. For the first five or ten minutes, Lib was stiff and embarrassed, but then she began to enjoy it, I could tell. She looked almost graceful, and she looked very happy. After a while, another boy came and cut in and Joseph found himself another partner. But they kept glancing at each other.

I spotted Mrs. Frederiksen, dancing with her old friend, their steps matched perfectly, both of them smiling. And then a boy tapped my shoulder and introduced himself as Daniel Darby. I told him I didn't know how to dance. He said he didn't, either. He just wanted to ask me questions about the race—he wanted to enter it next year. I liked talking to him. I liked telling him that my father had been a horse trainer—and it made me smile when he said I was the best rider he had ever seen.

The rest of the night went by to the tune of lively fiddles and the sound of laughter. And when it came time to go home, I rode Sarah at a walk, behind the wagon. Libby rode on the driver's bench with Mrs. Frederiksen, holding the lantern.

I put Sarah in Flynn's stall and sat with her a long while before I left. She smelled me all over twice more, then stood close while I stroked her neck. When I finally went back up the hill, the stars were bright overhead. I tiptoed in, afraid I would wake Libby. But she was sound asleep. She had left the lantern lit for me and I could see her face. She was smiling. I snuffed the lantern, then stood in the darkness, listening to my sister's breathing, then the sound of Mrs. Frederiksen turning in her bed, then the sigh of a breeze coming through the gap in the waxed paper on the window.

Every sound was familiar and a comfort to me. It had been a long day and I was really tired. And it was so good to be home.